I0523684

A MURDEROUS CLAMOUR AT REDCLIFF MANOR

Shiraz Jones Marine Rescue Mysteries
Book One

Dedicated to Sanja Ansell, Marine Rescue Volunteer,
who gave me the idea

Copyright

A Murderous Clamour at Redcliff Manor:
Shiraz Jones Marine Rescue Mysteries Book One

ISBN: 978-0-6451187-7-3
Imprint: The Cozy Cabin Press
10 9 8 7 6 5 4 3 2 1

CONTENTS

Shiraz Jones Marine Rescue Mysteries are set in England and written by an English author.

Enjoy the Englishness!

CHAPTER ONE

"Shiraz? Galloping galleons. What kind of name's that?"

I'm a tall girl, especially when wearing my Gucci wedges, but the man facing me had to be six foot three, and broad as well.

I tossed my long, dark-brown hair over my shoulder and met his eyes. "Um, it's my first name, sir. I'm Shiraz Jones, the new recruit. Would you be Mr Murphy? They told me to ask for you." I held out my hand, but he didn't take it.

The man stepped one pace forward, removed his rough, weathered fists from the pockets of his bright-yellow waterproofs and glanced down. "Don't call me Mr Murphy, and never call me Sir. None of this 'aye-aye' pirate rubbish in Redcliff Marine Rescue. My name's Murph, and that's how you'll refer to me."

My first day saving lives at sea, and already I've upset the boss.

He rubbed his bushy, brown beard and inspected me slowly, starting at my feet, still in the wedge shoes I'd jammed on when I couldn't find my runners.

I was accustomed to men looking me up and down, but this was a unique experience. Murph wasn't admiring my toned body.

His gaze moved to my black Gymshark, joggers, elevated again to my grey, zip-up, Nike exercise hoodie and settled on my long, dark-brown hair. I twisted my right index finger in my left clenched fist and elected to fill the silence.

"I do have boating experience, Mr Murphy; I mean, Murph. I've crewed my ex-husband's yacht."

Murph tilted his head and frowned. "How big was the yacht?"

"Massive. One of the largest in the harbour. It had two jet skis on the rear deck, eight double cabins and a fully stocked cocktail bar."

I swallowed, as I realised these might not be as impressive features to him as they'd been to my former husband's clients.

Murph slitted his eyes. "And when you say you crewed the yacht, what was your role, exactly?"

"Um, mainly to lie on the front deck dressed in a bikini and sailor hat, and wave at photographers." I clenched my teeth in a sheepish grin and decided I'd filled enough silences.

Murph puffed out an exaggerated breath. "Bloodthirsty barrelmen." He gesticulated with both palms. "Why would a lady with your background want to join our crew? This won't be one of your jolly bikini-and-cocktail boat rides. This is real-world stuff, a long way from the big city."

He jabbed his finger twice at the metal roller shutters which separated the boat shed from the small town's harbour. "Out there, we're dealing with people stuck in quicksand on an incoming tide, kite surfers blown miles out to sea, commercial fishing vessels which, for whatever reason, have decided not to be seaworthy anymore. We're saving lives. It's not easy, and it's not pretty. You'll witness desperate people who think they're about to die, terrified children screaming for their parents and apoplectic old ladies panicking because Fluffy the poodle's fallen in the waves and can't swim. You'll answer a shout to save a person in the water, which turns out to be an old overcoat. You'll answer another shout to save a person in the water, which turns out to be a dead body."

He paused and sighed. "D'you think you can handle all that? Because, if not, tell me now, and you'll save us both a lot of time and trouble."

This was a fair question. An average marine rescue recruit was probably tougher than me, rougher than me and didn't come with Chanel makeup, Versace sunglasses and Bulgari earrings.

I set my jaw, held my hands behind my back and crossed two sets of fingers. "I'm not that bikini-and-cocktail girl anymore. She's history. I've left her behind in the city, and

9

I've returned to Redcliff, where I holidayed as a little girl. I used to watch your boat from my bedroom window and dream of being a marine rescue volunteer but, as an eight-year-old, I didn't realise women could join. In those days, all the volunteers were men."

Murph shuffled his feet.

I planted my hands on my hips and looked him in the eyes. "I'm Shiraz Jones, your newest recruit, and I'm here to soak up whatever you can teach me, and whatever the sea throws at me."

Murph nodded minutely.

"Although,"—I smiled, held up my fingers and wiggled them—"I'd prefer if I didn't break a nail."

Murph furrowed his brow, then placed both hands on his stomach, tipped his head back and guffawed. I laughed with him, although I wasn't sure where the next part of this conversation would go. We were in uncharted waters here, and I didn't want to go down with my ship.

"Shiraz, here at Redcliff Marine Rescue, we'll train you in all aspects of water safety. We're an independent, charity-funded volunteer organisation, but that doesn't mean we're any less professional. We'll teach you how to handle lines, how to swim in a full dry suit, which, for your information, comes in a fetching colour of bright yellow, and we'll show you how to pull someone out of the sea without detaching their head from their body. If you wish to progress further, we'll teach you to drive the vessel and lead a team performing dangerous, complex rescues, quite literally saving lives at sea."

He paused and formed a straight line with his lips.

"You'll need to commit to a lot of training. One or two evenings a week in the classroom with me, and boat duties at weekends. You won't be able to attend emergencies until you've passed your qualified crew certificate, which could take over a year, depending on how quick a learner you are. Once you're proficient, you'll join the Search and Rescue team, and you won't be able to sit down for dinner or go for drinks with your friends without wondering whether your pager's going to go off."

He rifled through a folder and produced a piece of paper with the heading, 'Redcliff Marine Rescue: New Member Checklist.'

"If you're okay with that, and"—he laughed once—"you don't mind breaking the odd nail, then let's start with your vessel induction. Welcome to the crew."

And on that note, my life changed forever.

For the last twenty years, I'd held the coattails of a high-profile London personality. Montague Jones (or Monty, to the press) knew everybody, and everybody knew him. A public relations fixer, the adversary of the society pages, a man from whom the words 'no comment' were the most any reporter could hope to extract, there was no indiscretion too large for Monty to dissipate. No affair too brazen. No irregularity too irregular.

And for twenty years, every magazine photo of Monty, dressed immaculately in a bow tie, white dress shirt and ironed Levi's jeans included somebody else.

Someone slightly shorter than Monty, when he sported his brown, ankle-length, pointy cowboy boots with the two-inch lifts in the heels. I hated them.

Someone better-looking than Monty, if I say so myself.

Someone quieter than Monty, less obvious than Monty, and yet essential to the egotistical, narcissistic, Monty-centred modus operandi we all knew and expected.

Dutifully half a step behind him, her jewelled, manicured hand linked through the arm of his Armani jacket, Monty's permanent, trademark accessory smiled at the cameras, shook hands with those he wished to impress and performed her obligations without question.

Until I didn't want to be that girl anymore.

When we met, weeks after my eighteenth birthday, I gave up everything for him. My embryonic modelling career, a promise of a small part in a major motion picture, my boyfriend at the time who didn't deserve to be dumped for this man who was almost thirty years older than me.

But Monty guarded a secret.

A secret that Montague Jones PR successfully camouflaged for twenty years.

A secret, it seemed, several people knew, but I wasn't one of them.

Monty loved someone else all along.

Not me.

Not his society love, the ever-smiling, never-speaking, trophy-wife arm-candy.

No.

Monty's true love was his constant companion, hidden in plain sight.

His soulmate.

His personal assistant.

Darren.

And, when I discovered this, it was time for me to get out. You would've done the same, right? This was the catalyst for my decision to abandon my empty, meaningless city life and do something for me. I slammed the door on my city apartment, withdrew enough money from our joint bank account to keep me going for approximately ever and blew the first wad of cash on a taxi to Redcliff-upon-Sea.

No looking back.

Murph spent two hours showing me the rescue boat, which usually carried a crew of four, plus any unfortunate souls who needed assistance. Four, soon to include me. Wow! My mind buzzed with the information he'd given me, although my brain overflowed fifteen minutes into his presentation, and now I needed caffeine. Possibly intravenously.

A giant, illuminated, pink seashell hung above the building next door to the marine rescue boat shed. The Wicked Whelk café seemed to be the best, possibly the only, option for a mid-morning double-shot, soy latte. Somewhere to gather my thoughts about the sea-change I was experiencing. If you'll pardon the pun.

I smiled at the petite woman behind the counter as she carried two steaming mugs in her left hand and three plates containing heavenly smelling bacon sandwiches dripping with butter balancing up her right arm. Her short, blonde bob partly covered her round, pretty face. I reckoned she was younger than me. Maybe around thirty. Although, people mistook me for thirty. How many more years could I keep that up?

"Won't be a minute. D'you know what you want?" She swept out of the kitchen towards a table where three bearded, ruddy-faced men sat dressed in a uniform of faded, blue overalls. One of them glanced at me, nodded, then looked away.

Every table in the café contained similarly clothed people, and the noise of conversation competed with a radio playing golden oldies interspersed with local news, fish prices and weather reports. I turned around and watched condensation drip down the windows.

"There," said the lady, returning and resting her arms on the counter. "What can I get you?" She extracted a pencil from the top pocket of her apron.

"A soy latte, please. With an extra shot."

She spluttered and laughed. "Sorry, I don't have soy. There's not much call for it in Redcliff. I can do you an extra shot and skinny milk."

"Sure. Force of habit. I've ordered the same drink for years in London."

She tapped out the coffee, and the machine hissed. I inhaled the smell of the freshly ground beans and smiled.

"What brings you to Redcliff-upon-Sea?" she asked. "We don't see many tourists at this time of year."

"I'm not a tourist; I've moved here from the city. Newly separated; starting over. I've joined up with Redcliff Marine Rescue, next door." I nodded my head to the left, as she tapped the metal jug to settle the milk.

"We'll be working together, then. I enlisted last month. The coxswain's been trying to persuade me to volunteer for ages. Personally, I reckon he wants my contribution 'cos he thinks I'll be dishing out free bacon sandwiches."

I laughed. "Is the training hard? There must be a lot to learn."

"I've no idea. My first classroom session's tomorrow."

"Mine, too. We can share study notes." I held out my hand. "I'm Shiraz Jones."

"Shiraz? That's an unusual name. I've only seen it on a red wine label."

"It's Middle Eastern. My father's Egyptian, but I was brought up in England."

"It's nice to meet you. I'm Emily. Emily Philpot. Have you met Murph yet? The coxswain?"

"Yes. He gave me my induction this morning."

"He's a character, isn't he? Ex-navy. Terrible about his wife."

"Oh? What happened to her?"

"A tragedy. They were sea kayaking, and she drowned. It must've been ten years ago. She was such a lovely person; only thirty-five years old. Murph swore something good would come from her death, so he jumped into Marine Rescue with both feet, and now he dedicates all his spare time to saving lives at sea. He can be gruff, but he sets very high standards for himself, and expects everyone else to do the same."

The scraping of chairs announced a mass departure, and every table emptied as the fishermen and women drained coffees, stood and threw on waterproof jackets. A chorus of 'Bye, Emily,' echoed as an icy blast through the door accompanied their exit.

"Where are they all going?" I asked.

Emily pointed to a poster pinned to the wall entitled, 'Tide Tables: Headland Bay.' "Fishing. The tide must be turning."

She passed me my coffee, and I realised I had so much to learn, and I was, if you'll pardon yet another pun, well out of my depth.

Emily cleared tables while I sat and wrapped my hands around my warm drink. The steam wafted towards my nose, and I blew on the cup and took a sip of caffeine heaven. Life in the country meant I'd have to get used to cow's milk again.

The café door opened, and a slight, young girl wearing a coat with a fluff-edged hood entered. She closed the door slowly, so it made no sound, flipped the hood back and stood in the doorway. Her skin was white as paper, but her eyes were red and swollen, as if she'd been crying.

Emily looked up from clearing tables. "Can I help you?"

The girl glanced around, as if she didn't want anyone to recognise her. She stared through me, then turned back to Emily. "Are you serving drinks?"

Her accent seemed Eastern European, maybe Russian. I'd originally thought she was a teenager, but I now reckoned she was in her early twenties.

"Of course," said Emily. She laid down her cloth and approached the girl. "Is everything okay? You look upset. It's Katherine, isn't it?"

"Kateryna," said the girl. "Please, could I have a hot chocolate? And, if you have vodka, put two shots in it."

"Sorry," said Emily. "I don't have a licence to serve alcohol. I'll bring your hot chocolate. Take a seat." Emily glanced over at me and gave an expression of commiseration.

Kateryna plopped into a chair on a neighbouring table, laid her head on her arms and sobbed.

I couldn't ignore this, so I sat opposite her and touched her arm. "D'you want to talk to me? My name's Shiraz."

She raised her head. She'd been rubbing her eyes so hard the black circles around her red, bloodshot irises resembled a Terence Conran saucer design. Her mascara ran down her cheeks in two vertical lines. She covered her mouth with both hands, and I watched her body convulse while the tears flowed.

"Please tell me what's wrong." I squeezed her hand. "I'm a good listener."

Her voice, when it came, was a whisper, and I leant forward to hear her.

"My family must never, ever know. I can't live with this any longer. I want to kill myself."

"What? What's wrong?"

She paused and exhaled.

"I'm pregnant."

I recoiled. This didn't come in the moving-to-the-country training manual. I'd had to deal with anorexic models telling me their life wasn't worth living because their picture hadn't appeared in this month's *Red Carpet Superstars* magazine, but I knew they were being dramatic. I didn't think this girl was, although, beneath the messed-up hair and smeared makeup, she had the high cheekbones and full lips so prized by fashion photographers.

"Don't tell anyone, okay?" She clenched her teeth. "None of them must know."

Emily brought her drink and mouthed 'Okay?' to me. I pinched my lips and shrugged.

Right now, I had in front of me a young woman I'd never met, considering suicide, and I'd no idea what to do, or what to say.

So I said nothing.

Kateryna clutched her hot chocolate and stared into the frothy milk. This was a good start. She couldn't kill herself while both hands were around a white, pottery mug. She met my eyes.

"I have to end my life," she continued. "What else can I do?"

My relief that she'd spoken without me prompting her felt like an enormous lump dropping inside my stomach, and I continued to employ the tactic of not filling her silence.

Just leaning towards her.

Then she forced me to speak.

"What would you do?" she asked.

And with those four words, she transported me back twenty years.

CHAPTER TWO

Kateryna's question took me back to my central London apartment, where I'd lived with four other girls aged between sixteen and twenty-two, all believing we'd be the next Kate Moss.

None of us would be.

At the time, none of us knew that.

Except me. Eighteen years old, and I was pregnant. One big, fat nail in my catwalk dreams.

I knew who the father was, but I couldn't tell him. I couldn't tell anybody. It would've ruined him; the scandal of a married, forty-year-old family television presenter. We'd met when he interviewed me after my biggest success, a double page spread in *Red Carpet Superstars* about life as an aspiring supermodel. He took me out to dinner, ostensibly to discuss an entire show about teenage girls trying to succeed in the big, bad modelling world, where every calorie counted, every pose mattered, and every predator had to be satisfied.

Eighteen-year-old me loved the attention, talking about myself for two hours. Any teenager would've been the same, right?

And then he got me pregnant.

I knew it was him, because there hadn't been anyone else.

Ever.

My career was over before it had begun. I couldn't disclose my pregnancy to my friends, my parents or my flatmates.

So I spoke with the one person I could confide in.

The one person I could trust with my secret, as she didn't move in the same circles as the people who mattered to my insecure self-image.

The only person who'd listen.

And once I'd sat on the floor with my arms around my knees and poured out my heart to our middle-aged, Caribbean cleaner, she'd told me about another place she worked where they could help my problem go away.

Montague Jones PR.

And we all know how that ended up. But enough about me.

Because, right now, I needed to recall what had solved my own problem all those years ago and see if I could employ those memories to help the desperate young woman seated in front of me.

Emily dumped a pile of paper napkins on the table. I mouthed 'thank you' and passed one to Kateryna, who smeared more eye makeup over her cheeks.

"I know how you feel." As soon as I said this, it sounded trite, so I told her something I hadn't discussed with anyone for twenty years.

"I was pregnant myself at eighteen."

"Eighteen?" Kateryna's mouth fell open. "What did you do?"

"I'll tell you what I didn't do. I didn't kill myself. Obviously. Feel me. I'm real; I'm not a ghost." I grabbed her hand and held it against my arm.

The teeniest, tiniest smile formed at the corner of her mouth, then disappeared.

"The question is," I said, "what are we going to do with you?"

And with the word 'we', Kateryna's expression relaxed slightly, and I hoped I'd diverted her suicidal thoughts.

The café door swung open, and a short, thin, middle-aged man approached Emily, who was stacking a dishwasher behind the counter. He didn't glance our way, but Kateryna saw him and pulled her hood up.

"He can't notice me here," she said. "I'm supposed to be at a medical appointment." She ducked to make herself invisible but, as we were the only two people in the café, this ploy was risky at best.

Then she stood and headed for the exit, and I had no choice but to dump my half-finished coffee and follow her. Because I'd never have forgiven myself if she'd carried out her threat, and I could've helped her, talked to her, offered a friendly shoulder to cry on.

Day two in Redcliff-upon-Sea, and now I'm a Samaritan?

Kateryna hurried away from the café with her head down, and I marched to catch up.

"Hold up." I winced as I stumbled and hurt my ankle. "I'm not wearing the right footwear for sprinting." I glanced over my shoulder. "Who was that man in the café? Why did you need to get away from him?"

So many questions.

No answers.

"We can't go through town," she said. "No one must see me. We'll walk along the beach away from the harbour then up the cliffs."

"Um, okay." I speed-marched after her and hoped my footwear would cope with wherever she led me.

The two of us jumped down from the path at the end of the harbour wall, and the shingle crunched as we landed on the beach.

I grabbed her arm. "Stop."

She turned around and faced me, and I put both hands on her shoulders. "There's no one around. It's cold, drizzly and I can't run in these shoes. What are you escaping? Start at the beginning. Tell me."

Kateryna sighed. She placed one hand on the top edge of her belly and one below and breathed slowly. Her gesture reminded me of how I'd performed the same action when I had a small human growing inside me.

"I'm from Ukraine."

That's where your accent comes from.

"My parents, they're not well. And they are poor people; they have little. They sent me away to escape the war. One of my brothers is fighting the Russians, the other,"—her voice cracked—"his fight is over.

My father said he'd lost one son; he might lose another. He couldn't face losing all his children."

She paused. "There's a charity. A charity which assists Ukrainian women and children. They help them flee the country and live somewhere safer."

We took position side by side, strolling along the beach with our hands in our pockets. The rain had stopped, and a weak sun attempted to shine through gaps in a grey cloud. Anyone seeing us would've thought we were two old friends enjoying conversation.

Not two people who'd met five minutes ago, one of whom was trying to keep the other's mind off suicide.

"So the charity brought me here. The lady who runs it, Elizabeth Bramhall, she has a house called Redcliff Manor. She owns horses. I had a horse in Ukraine. And I nearly finished my accountant studies before the war started. When Mrs Bramhall discovered this, she arranged for me to work at her house. They needed someone to keep their accounts. And someone to look after their horses. I do both."

"I studied accounting at school too," I said. "I loved it. But life took another turn. Things would've been very different if I'd become an accountant."

"At Redcliff Manor, they still do the books by hand. No computer. Can you believe that? Even in Ukraine we used a computer."

Kateryna stopped and glanced over her shoulder. We were the only people on the beach, apart from a distant figure walking a dog. I heard three sharp barks carry across the water.

"How long have you lived here?" I asked, in a desperate attempt to keep her mind on her story. "Is Mrs Bramhall nice to you?"

"I've been here six months. But Mrs Bramhall, she's never here. She lives in an apartment in London."

"What? You're on your own, looking after her horses?"

"No. Not alone. I live with"—she spat—"them."

I puffed. "Kateryna, I arrived in Redcliff-upon-Sea yesterday. I haven't met anyone except a man at Redcliff Marine Rescue station, the woman who runs the café, and now you. Who is 'them'?"

"Them. Them is Grantley Bramhall, Elizabeth's husband, although you never see them together, their son Charlie and two staff members."

"Who was the man in the café? Was that Grantley whoever?"

"Him?" She spat again. "He's nothing. That's Nigel. He's Mr Bramhall's secretary, butler, chauffeur, whatever-er. I hate him. I hate all of them."

She turned inland from the beach and ascended a steep path framed with small trees and wild, scratchy blackberry bushes. I followed her and gave up on my shoes ever surviving this experience. Goodness knows where I'd buy a replacement pair of Gucci wedges in Redcliff.

"Kateryna, wait. Wait for me."

27

She strode ahead, and I realised she'd taken this route many times; she knew every bend, every uneven step, every exposed tree root. I struggled to keep sight of her. She wasn't my problem, but she'd become my problem, and I'd have been devastated if she did what she threatened, and I'd been the last person to see her.

Plus, she intrigued me.

I wanted to hear her story.

I wanted to understand her.

Because she was the younger me.

We burst out into a meadow at the top of the cliffs. Kateryna paused and turned around.

I planted my hands on my knees, bent over and puffed.

"Come on." Kateryna beckoned me and set off along the edge of the meadow. "We don't have long."

Don't have long until what? You take your own life?

I inhaled deeply and caught up with her. "Why do you hate all of them?"

"They see me as the hired help. A serving girl. The lowest. No one at Redcliff Manor talks to me. Unless they want me to do something for them. I love the horses. They listen."

We walked out onto a small promontory and stopped close to the edge of a cliff. The cloud had lifted, and the sea stretched to the horizon. I noticed five distant boats, and wondered if these were the fishers from the café. Distant diagonals of rain patched across the water. I took a step forward and gazed downward. To my left, I saw the beach we'd walked along, and the town behind it. The dog I'd noticed earlier barked and chased a stick thrown by its owner. To my right, a smaller, secluded, half-moon bay lay partly hidden. I peered down at it and reckoned it wasn't accessible by foot; the promontory we stood on prevented that. A landslip fanned down from the cliff and covered some of the oval, grey pebbles.

To my horror, Kateryna walked to the edge and sat, her legs dangling over the precipice.

"No!" I yelled. "Talk to me first." I peeped over, swallowed hard and crouched behind her. No way was I hanging over a cliff, swinging my legs fifty feet up. The last thing I wanted was to kill myself while trying to prevent her from doing the same.

She glanced at me over her shoulder. "This is my special place. I come here, watch the waves and talk to the birds." She pointed at two gulls circling above the water. "The beach down there, West Cove. Nobody can walk to it except at the lowest tides. And at high tide, the waves crash against the cliff below, and go whump...whump...whump. I can hear them from my bedroom on stormy nights. Then I walk out in the moonlight and feel the wind on my face, taste the salt air. It's my only escape." She clenched her teeth. "I hate this town. Hate it. I hate everything."

Kateryna swung her legs and bashed her ankles together. I really needed to get her off this cliff edge.

She turned around to look at me.

I saw something in her eyes and thought she'd push herself off the cliff, so I grabbed her around the waist.

She wriggled out of my grip, stood and brushed herself off. "You're just like all the rest of them. Leave me alone." She turned around and sprinted across the meadow behind us.

I panted and pushed myself to my feet. Running after her wasn't going to be an option in my wedges, and there was no way in this cold weather I'd take them off and go barefoot. The relief I'd prevented her from launching herself onto the beach below swept over me. I stared after her, but she'd gone, and the only noise remaining was the cries of the gulls.

Now what do I do?

Evening damp drew in, and I pulled my coat around my face as I walked back along the seafront to my accommodation, Melville Cottage, opposite Redcliff's main beach. My feet, I was sure, had frostbite.

Who goes to a marine rescue induction, then walks up a cliff in wedges?

As soon as I opened the door, I pressed the button on the kettle, made a cup of instant coffee, which tastes disgusting, by the way, and sat at the kitchen table, mesmerised by the steam rising from the mug.

What just happened to me?

I'd arrived in town yesterday, met the burly, surly marine rescue coxswain this morning, introduced myself to one of my new colleagues who also ran the local café and, within ten minutes, found myself on the edge of a cliff, trying to talk a pregnant girl out of jumping.

My London life hadn't been this complicated. All I'd had to do was put on a stunning dress, killer heels and expensive makeup, hop in the back of the Rolls Royce, step out at some film premiere and wave to the cameras. That was easy-peasy. What had I done?

I jumped and dashed to the window, as the wail of a siren pierced the air.

CHAPTER THREE

From my accommodation window, I gazed at the lights of the harbour and the marine rescue station, perched next to the Wicked Whelk café. A flashing red light strobed from the building, and floodlights illuminated miniature figures surrounding the rescue vessel as its tractor towed it to the water. One of them must've been Murph from the outline, but I wasn't sure who the other two were.

Very soon, that'd be me in the bright-yellow, horrendously unfashionable waterproofs. Seriously, they'd probably be the most practical clothes I'd ever worn.

As soon as the boat launched, I watched its lights leave the harbour, speed towards the horizon and disappear around the nearby promontory.

My coffee waited on the table, and I circled the mug with my hands and thought about Kateryna.

Where was she now? Was she safely back wherever she lived?

Why did she hate the people she lived with?

It didn't sound like they treated her with any respect; she'd said they barely spoke to her unless they wanted something, but 'hate' is a strong word.

She had a home where no one was dropping bombs on her, although she must be worried sick about her family in Ukraine. Especially her surviving brother.

I knew what it was like to be pregnant and far from home.

Too afraid to tell anyone.

A smile formed; she'd confided in me.

How can I help you? I don't know you. Why do you feel desperate enough to want to kill yourself?

I made up my mind. Tomorrow morning, I'd return to the café and ask Emily about Kateryna.

For now, I had my own needs to think of. I unlocked my phone and downloaded a document entitled 'Marine Rescue Student Workbook'.

216 pages? Seriously?

"Where is everyone?" I asked Emily the next day, as I closed the café door behind me and gazed at the empty tables.

She glanced up from behind the counter, where the noise of a dishwasher suddenly ended. She opened the door, and the machine billowed a spectacular cumulonimbus of steam across the ceiling.

"Morning, Shiraz. I have got your name right, haven't I? I knew it was a type of wine."

I smiled. "You have. And I remember you're called Emily."

"Well done. Same coffee as yesterday; double-shot, skinny latte? But without soy milk?" She grinned.

"Gosh, you have a good memory. Yes, please."

The coffee machine hissed and bubbled as she wiped the spout and sterilised the milk jug with steam. "The fishermen aren't here yet. Morning rush'll be in an hour or so. They come in for their hot drinks and sandwiches before setting off for the day."

Emily tapped out the coffee container. "What happened yesterday? You'd barely finished your drink before you dashed out of here with that girl. She looked very upset. Had you met before?"

"Never. I didn't know anyone in Redcliff until I arrived two days ago. D'you know her?"

"She comes in every Saturday to take an order of pastries to the manor. But she's never been in during the week. Her name's something like Katherine."

"It's Kateryna. She's from Ukraine. I found out that much." I paused and bit my bottom lip. "She's in deep trouble, and I want to help her. Where can I find her?"

"She works at Redcliff Manor. That's all I know. What kind of trouble's she in?"

My memory cast back to the days of my own teenage pregnancy, and how I desperately didn't want anyone to know. Emily seemed nice, but there was a chance I was about to spill Kateryna's secret to the town gossip.

"Um, she has family problems."

There. That wasn't exactly lying, was it?

Emily poured my coffee, chocolate-dusted the top with a whelk pattern, then emptied small plates from the dishwasher into a cupboard. She stood, held the small of her back with one hand, and wiped her forehead with the other.

"Are you okay?" I asked.

"I've been on the go since 5:00 a.m. There's only another six hours until I close up at 2:00. And then there's marine rescue training this evening. I'll have a nap this afternoon."

I grabbed her forearm as she crashed a basket of cutlery onto the worktop. "Sit down with me. I'll help you clear up afterwards. How will I get through this evening's training if my colleagues are collapsing?"

Plus, I want the inside track on what goes on at Redcliff Manor.

"I need a break." Emily undid her chalkboard-grey apron and hung it on a hook. "Grab a seat, and I'll make myself a drink and join you."

The wooden chair scraped on the lino floor as I pulled it away from a table for two and sat in the same place I'd sat yesterday.

Before my unplanned sprint up the cliff path.

Before my desperate conversation with a suicidal girl.

Emily placed her cup on the table, pulled her chair out and sat. She pushed her blonde bob out of her eyes and stirred her coffee. "Running this place by myself is a big job. I used to have a woman who helped me part-time, but her husband broke his pelvis falling off the harbour wall onto his fishing boat. She cares for him now and doesn't have time to help me." She glanced up. "So how are you doing? Finding your way?"

"Yes, doing fine. Although yesterday's events left me rather shaken." I took a deep breath.

Here we go, Shiraz. Jump in with both feet.

"You said Kateryna works at Redcliff Manor. Do you, um, know the people there?"

"Grantley Bramhall owns the place. New money. People say he made a fortune selling dodgy city investments. Two years ago, he swept in and bought the manor from the old lady who lived there by herself. Poor dear, she couldn't afford to pay the rates, let alone maintain the place. He rocked up with his brand-new Rolls Royce and his wads of cash and, between you and me, I reckon she was delighted to offload it. Since then, there's been a constant stream of builders coming and going, which has been great for my

36

takeaway business. His renovations must be finished now. I don't see them anymore."

She paused and sipped her coffee. Gosh, this was an enjoyable chat. Years had passed since I'd sat and talked with a female friend without walking on eggshells in case they had another agenda.

I pursed my lips. I needed to find out as much information as I could before Emily returned to her kitchen. Anything could help me understand what Kateryna was going through. "Who else lives at Redcliff Manor? Kateryna mentioned Grantley had a son."

"Pah. You mean Charlie. Lazy, good-for-nothing, entitled brat. Twenty-three years old, and he'll never need to work in his life. He spends his days driving his Ferrari between his parents' homes, from here to the city and back. If you need an example of how wealth destroys people, take a look at Charlie."

My mind flashed back to my own days in London, when I careered around in a convertible pink Porsche, and I decided Emily didn't need to know that aspect of my background.

"Ppff." I rolled my eyes. "I know the type. Family money, flash car, selection of pretty girls in the passenger seat."

Emily leant towards me. Even though we were the only people in the café, she whispered. "Rumour has it, he's promised to Alexandra Flaxworth-Mills. She's in her late twenties; private school educated. She's not Charlie's type; she doesn't have a model figure, and she's not exactly pretty, but she does have one characteristic which would serve Grantley well."

"Oh? What's that?"

"Her father's a knight, and he sits in parliament."

"Her father's in government? What advantage would that be to Grantley?"

"Respectability. Status. He thought he could swan into Redcliff-upon-Sea, buy the manor and instantly become the local squire, respected and admired by everyone. He's discovering that possessing boatloads of cash isn't enough to impress the folk here. But if his son married into the local titled family, people from a wealthy lineage who've lived here for generations, he believes he'd gain the status which is eluding him."

The café door opened, and a cold breeze accompanied it.

"Excuse me," said Emily. She stood. A glance over my shoulder revealed the back of the man I'd seen yesterday; the one Kateryna had wanted to avoid. I frowned and watched as he bought several items from Emily, accepted them wrapped in paper bags and left without looking my way.

What did Kateryna say his name was?

Emily returned. "I've enjoyed our chat, but I must start preparing for the fishers." She darted a glance at the clock. "They'll be here any minute."

At that point, Murph's figure filled the entrance. He slammed the door behind him, and I winced, thinking the panes of glass would drop out of the frame.

"One coffee, please, Emily, and one of your finest bacon sandwiches." He noticed me. "Rollicking reef knots. Here's Shiraz as well. I hope you two are brushing up for training tonight."

"I saw you had a shout yesterday evening," I said, pausing to see his reaction at my use of the word 'shout'. "I watched the boat from my window. What was the job?"

Job? Shout? What are you becoming, Shiraz?

Murph placed his flat palms on the table opposite me, looked down at them and shook his head. "Not pleasant. I'm glad we don't have to deal with that too often."

"Deal with what?"

He looked up.

"Dead body."

CHAPTER FOUR

I stared at Murph with my mouth open. "Dead body?"

"Yep. When the pager went off yesterday, I honestly thought it was another false alarm. Who goes in the water in midwinter?"

"Where were they? Out at sea somewhere?"

"On the beach at West Cove. A man walking his dog saw it from the clifftop."

A chill started at my stomach and fanned outward.

Murph continued. "It wasn't the usual south-westerly last night, so we could beach the boat, but when we arrived, we knew it was too late. The Coastguard took them away in a body bag."

"Did you see the body? Do you know them?"

"Young female. Long, blonde hair, seriously injured. She must've fallen from the cliff; there's no other way to reach West Cove at high tide."

"Poor girl," said Emily. "Those cliffs are dangerous. I've often said there should be a fence along the edge."

"There was a fence, once. When the big landslide happened fifteen years ago, it took the fence with it, and it's never been replaced." Murph bit into his food, and tomato ketchup squirted out of the side. "The bacon sandwiches are good today, Emily. Could I have some more sauce?"

Their conversation blurred into the background.

My tears came, because I knew whose body it was, and I could've saved her.

But I hadn't.

That evening, Emily grabbed hold of me the minute I sat down in the training room. Murph stood at the front fighting with his laptop, a device I figured he was less familiar with than the controls on the rescue boat. A man in his thirties with tightly curled, brown hair leant over the computer, clicked the mouse and pointed, as the display at the front of the room showed a logo above the words 'Basic Training Course'. Murph thanked him, and he strode through the training room and departed via a door behind us. I craned my neck to watch him leave.

"Shiraz," said Emily. "I need to talk to you."

My man-curiosity evaporated. "What?"

"The body they found. It was Kateryna, the girl you spoke with yesterday."

"I knew it. She seemed so upset. I tried to talk her out of it. Then she ran off and must've returned to the cliff later and jumped.

I should've gone after her. I should've helped her. And now she's dead, and I can't."

A silent tear ran down my cheek.

Murph's voice boomed from the front of the room. "Good evening, everyone. Welcome to tonight's marine rescue training, the first session for all of you. I'll circulate course notes, and you'll each receive a keyring as a thank you for joining." He dangled a red, metal circle.

Emily passed me a tissue, and I wiped my eyes and spread makeup liberally around my face. She made a 'shh' signal and whispered, "Let's talk afterwards."

Murph began speaking about his computer presentation. Each slide depicted a different piece of safety equipment or clothing, and he held up examples and pointed out features.

His words floated over my head.

I should've done more for Kateryna. The girl was a long way from her family and any support they could give her.

Boy, did I know how that felt.

She'd even told me she wanted to kill herself, in the café, when we'd met. Then she'd led me on the scarper up the cliff path and out to her favourite place where she sat to watch the waves and the gulls.

I replayed our conversation as best I could, given I was panicking she'd throw herself off the cliff right there and then.

Murph's voice intruded on my thoughts. "Shiraz, in an emergency, when would you use a red distress flare to attract attention, as opposed to an orange smoke flare?"

I looked up, and the rest of the class turned towards me.

"Um..."

Emily nudged my elbow and whispered, "After dark."

"After dark," I shouted.

Murph pursed his lips and nodded slowly. "Thank you, Shiraz. I'm sorry to have disturbed your daydreaming."

I glanced into my lap and felt my cheeks tingle and turn the colour of stop lights.

As soon as Murph finished presenting the final slide, I grabbed Emily's arm. "Can we talk? About Kateryna?"

"Not here. Outside."

I threw my coat on and chased after her.

"Would you like a glass of wine?" asked Emily. "I can relax tonight; it's Sunday tomorrow. The café's closed."

"Um, sure."

"Great. Let's go to my place." She unlocked a door to the side of the Wicked Whelk.

"You live above the café?"

"I do. Come on up."

We ascended a narrow, straight staircase and popped up like moles into the centre of a small room framed with dark, exposed, timber beams. A kitchen counter decorated the wall to my left, and a small dining table for two, a sofa and a bookcase overflowing paperbacks filled the rest of the room. Emily must've left the heating on while we were at training, and I shed my coat and draped it over the furniture.

A large ginger cat ba-doomphed off a window ledge and rubbed itself around Emily's legs, purring like a well-serviced lawn mower.

Emily laughed. "Hang on, Boots. Let me sort myself out, then I'll feed you."

"He's gorgeous," I said, bending to stroke the cat. "Is that his name, Boots? How cute."

"Yep. Murph found him as a kitten in the marine rescue station, hiding in one of the crew's boots." She rolled her eyes. "Hence the name. He lives at the station, but he seems to have moved in with me too. He's our communal kitty." She forked mince from a Tupperware container and set a bowl down. "He's a greedy guts. He knows exactly when the fishing fleet's due and stands on the dock waiting for them, twitching his tail. He's aware he'll get scraps off every boat."

Boots gobbled the mince and hopped onto the couch. He pawed at a blanket, then curled up against a cushion and purred.

"I like his company," said Emily. "Especially on stormy nights." She grabbed a bottle from the kitchen bench, poured two glasses and handed me one. "Merlot. I prefer red in winter."

"Me too." I set down the glass, pulled out a dining chair and plopped onto it.

Emily sat opposite me, and we clinked glasses.

"Cheers," she said. "Welcome to Redcliff-upon-Sea. Although, it's been a baptism of fire for you, hasn't it?"

I stared around the room and sighed heavily. "As a young girl, I came here on holiday every year with my parents. We rented a wooden cabin. Same place; same week, every year. My dad was like that."

Emily smiled, then took a sip of wine.

"We visited your café then," I said, "but it was called something else. Not the Wicked Whelk."

"The Lobster Pot. I renamed it when I took over five years ago. So now you're back?"

"It's a long story. Since my teenage years, I've lived in London. I've been married and unmarried. I'm back here to be me, to be Shiraz Jones, not Monty Jones' arm-candy, or

Monty Jones' sidekick, or Monty Jones' stupid, blind, idiot bimbo." I tipped back the wine, and Emily quietly poured me a second glass.

"This Monty Jones was your husband?"

"Yep. Until I found out he'd been sleeping with his secretary for roughly the whole of our marriage."

"Poor you. Did you know her?'

"Him."

"Ah. Got it. Um, will you revert to your maiden name?"

"I'm not sure. Murph seemed to have enough problems with my first name. How d'you think he'd go with Shiraz Al-Khatib-Islambouli?"

I threw my head back and laughed.

Goodness, it's lovely to talk.

Emily formed a straight line with her lips. "Maybe keep Jones."

"I think so." I sipped the second glass of Merlot, which was going down rather too nicely. "Can we talk about Kateryna now?"

"Of course. Absolutely tragic." Emily shook her head. "I only ever saw her when she popped in to collect pastries at weekends. I can't believe she's dead."

"No. Such a pretty girl, under the tears and messed-up hair."

We both jumped at three loud thumps on the front door.

Emily glanced at her kitchen clock. "There's only one person who knocks like that," she said, as she clumped down the stairs to the front door, pursued by Boots, who'd decided the hour had come for an evening stroll.

I heard a man's voice. "Sorry to trouble you at this time in the evening, Emily. My power's out, and I wondered if I could borrow a torch?"

"It's no trouble, Oscar. Come in, and I'll introduce you to Shiraz."

She appeared at the top of the stairs followed by a fit-looking older man wearing a Macintosh and trilby hat. I stood as he paused at the top.

"No, no, don't get up," he said. "I won't be staying long."

"Nonsense, Oscar," said Emily. "Shiraz and I were sharing a bottle of wine. Take a seat and join us."

"Very well. That would be pleasant. It's a cold night." He sat in Emily's seat, and she joined us on a kitchen stool and tipped the bottom of the bottle into a third glass.

"This is my new friend, Shiraz." Emily introduced us.

"It's a pleasure to meet you, Shiraz. What a wonderful name." Oscar sipped his drink. "I think if I had my time again, I'd name my three sons after fine wines."

"Oscar Wainwright," said Emily, placing one hand on the man's shoulder, "is a stalwart of Redcliff Marine Rescue. He used to be the leading coxswain, as well as the town policeman."

"Gosh." I raised my eyebrows.

"I don't do much these days," said Oscar. "I'm retired from active service; the volunteer gift shop demands my time now. I'm happy to be able to contribute still. Not that we open in winter. No tourists."

Emily leant forward. "You've always got an ear to the ground, Oscar. What d'you know about last night's events?"

"Poor girl. Those cliffs are so dangerous. They always have been. I remember when I was a boy, one of my father's friends lost his dog there. Silly animal was pursuing a rabbit and chased it right over. Why on earth would anyone walk so close to the edge, they risk falling off?"

"She didn't fall," I said. "She jumped. I met the girl yesterday, and she was suicidal. Emily saw her too. I ran after her up the cliff path and had to persuade her not to kill herself right there and then. She must've returned later and leapt when,"—my voice faltered—"when no one was present to talk her out of it."

The three of us sat silently.

Oscar glanced up. "Her young man must be terribly upset."

CHAPTER FIVE

"Young man?" I asked. "D'you mean a boyfriend? Actually, she did tell me she was..." I stopped myself. Kateryna had asked me to keep her pregnant status under wraps.

"Was what?" asked Emily.

Quick, think of something.

"...wasn't seeing anyone. She told me she wasn't seeing anyone. So whoever this boyfriend is, she didn't want to admit to him."

Phew. Get out of jail card played.

"Strange," said Oscar. "I don't think it's a secret. He's Peter Rawlings' lad, Josh, who works with his dad on their fishing boat. I wonder if he knows yet?"

I wonder if he knows he had an unborn child?

Oscar stood. "Anyway, thank you for your hospitality. I'd better get back with this torch. My wife'll be sitting in the dark wondering where I am."

"Oops." Emily giggled, then made a serious face as she remembered what we'd been discussing.

"I should leave as well." I drained my glass. "A lot's happened today. Thank you so much for making me feel welcome. I'm over the moon we'll be training together. Let me give you my phone number; we can compare notes."

Emily passed me her phone, and I entered: 'Shiraz Jones: 07700 900119'.

We made our way down the steep stairs. Emily opened the door at the bottom, and discovered Boots waiting to come back in.

"Hello, Boots," said Oscar. He reached down to pat the cat. "It's a good job I didn't bring Cadbury tonight."

"Who's Cadbury?" I asked.

"My dog. He's a chocolate Labrador, hence the name."

"Cadbury, the chocolate Labrador. Love it. I can't wait to meet him."

Emily picked up a round, chipped bowl resting outside her front door. "Goodness, Boots, I need to fill your water dish. It looks like other cats and dogs have been helping themselves."

She turned to Oscar and me. "I leave this old café serving dish outside for him to drink from. But he's very good at sharing."

She ruffled the cat's ears. "Aren't you, Boots?"

Boots miaowed in agreement and rubbed against her legs.

"Goodnight, Emily," said Oscar. He held up the torch. "Thanks for this. I'll bring it back when they fix my power."

"Are you walking my way?" I asked him, not least because I would've preferred not to walk alone at 9:30 on a dark, winter's evening.

"Only briefly. My house is one row back from the harbour." He pointed up a narrow passageway between two thatched cottages.

"Okay. Goodnight, Oscar. Goodnight, Emily."

"Goodnight, Shiraz, fellow rescue hero." Emily waved Boots' paw from where he lay like a baby in her arms and closed the door. Oscar stumped home, and I put my head down and marched along the seafront to Melville Cottage.

The following day had a definite Sunday morning feel. Calling seagulls woke me, and I snuggled under my covers, in raptures at the cosyness of being warm and safe in my bed while, only a few yards outside, a brisk breeze blew, flipping the water into choppy waves.

But I can't stay in bed all day, right? Not like I used to in London, before putting on the glitzy, ritzy outfits and heading out to be fashionably late for a party with people I didn't care if I never saw again. Nope. This is new Shiraz: determined, strong, superwoman. I leapt out of bed, threw open the curtains and stared at the sea.

No boats. Not today. Maybe the fishermen took Sunday off? I reckoned that might be unlikely; the fish didn't work to a nine-to-five roster.

I glanced to the right and watched activity at the marine rescue station. Four volunteers wore identical, head-to-toe, yellow dry suits, the same type Murph had showed me at my induction. I couldn't tell who they were from this distance, but I knew they'd be headed out on weekend boat training. The siren would've gone off if this was a shout.

I considered striding over to the Wicked Whelk for my morning coffee, then remembered it would be closed today. Emily's day off. Where do the fishermen find their bacon sandwiches on Sundays?

I decided to take a stroll to find out.

The town centre felt eerily empty at 9:30 on this weekend morning. Two elderly ladies shuffled past on the opposite pavement, maybe heading for the morning church service. Leaves blew in a mini-whirlwind and settled in a doorway. Every shop had a sign saying 'closed', except for a small store selling newspapers, magazines and chocolate. I wrapped my coat around myself, tugged my woolly hat over my ears and continued up the main street, winding away from the seafront. The shops petered out, and hedges formed the boundary to the road out of town. I paused at a battered signpost which pointed up a winding lane. One finger of the sign had rusted and broken off, so all that could be read from the stump was 'AL'. Another finger was in better condition and pointed back the way I'd come from. It said 'Town Centre'.

The third finger's embossed letters had long since lost their paint, but from my position directly under the sign I could see they read 'Redcliff Manor'.

Redcliff Manor.

Kateryna's refuge from war in Ukraine.

Some refuge. She'd have been better off staying with her parents.

I glanced up the narrow lane, bordered by thick hedges on both sides. A bend concealed any building which it led to.

Light drizzle started, so I turned around and headed back through the town.

As I passed the newspaper shop, on impulse, I dropped in and bought a copy of the national paper. As is always the case with Sunday editions, it weighed around ten pounds and contained multiple colour supplements, most of which held no interest to me.

Who needed to know the life history of some 1960s fashion designer whose work had become trendy again? Not me anymore.

I did wonder if the paper would say anything about Kateryna's death, but it was far too unwieldy to read in the street, so I decided to save it for when I reached home.

The drizzle morphed into a damp mist, and I strode back to Melville Cottage.

In the absence of a double shot skinny latte from the Wicked Whelk, I forced myself to drink a cup made from instant granules, sat down and perused the paper. The front page contained an article about a philandering television star, a doom-and-gloom update on the cost-of-living crisis and a feel-good piece about some celebrity couple. I gazed at the photo of the thirty-somethings and realised, not too long ago, that would've been me.

The shrill buzz of my mobile phone sounded, and I jumped, then looked around and hoped I could find the device before the sixth ring. After five diddle-dees, I snatched it from the top of the microwave.

"Hello?"

"Shiraz? Is that you? It's Emily. I need to talk."

"Hi, Emily, is everything okay?"

"Are you at home? Can I come around? There's something you need to know. And I have to tell you face to face."

CHAPTER SIX

Emily rang the bell five minutes later, and I opened the door to find her red faced and out of breath.

"Come in," I said. "Did you run here? You look worn out."

"I...*puff*...sprinted. You...*puff*...have to hear this. D'you remember Oscar?" She panted and held her chest.

"The man from last night? Of course."

"I bumped into him this morning, walking Cadbury. And he told me the police have arrested a suspect."

"What d'you mean, arrested?" I shrugged. "Suspect for what?"

Emily pulled out a kitchen chair and collapsed into it. I cautiously sat opposite her.

"A suspect for the murder."

"What murder?" I held both hands up. "What are you talking about?"

"Kateryna. The Ukrainian girl who died the day before yesterday."

I shook my head vigorously. "She wasn't murdered. She told me she was going to kill herself. She committed suicide."

Emily wagged one finger left and right. "Uh-uh. The police say she was murdered."

"Really?" I made a face. "What makes them think that? And who have they arrested?"

"I don't know, is the answer to your first question, and as to your second, Oscar told me they'd arrested Josh Rawlings."

"Josh Rawlings? The boy who Oscar described as Kateryna's partner?"

"Correct. I can't believe it. I've known Josh all his life. He's a simple soul, gentle as anything. He wouldn't hurt a mouse, let alone kill another human. I can't imagine him stealing a toffee. If you genuinely believe she killed herself, we should tell the police. You might have important evidence to stop an innocent lad being charged. Josh'll never be able to defend himself."

"Hang on. Stop." I slapped the table. "Let's recap before we run off to the police. I don't want to look stupid. First, what do we know about Kateryna?"

I grabbed a pen and paper and headed it 'Kateryna'. "One: she's a refugee from Ukraine. She's lived here a few months."

Emily leant forward across the table. "Two: she lived and worked at Redcliff Manor."

"Redcliff Manor." I wrote it down. "Three: she had a boyfriend called Josh. Who you've known all his life and isn't the sharpest tool in the box."

"Right. But a lovely chap who definitely didn't murder her and will be absolutely terrified in police custody."

"Okay. We've established that. Four: Kateryna told me yesterday she hated this town, she hated everyone, and she was going to kill herself."

"Did she say why she was so upset? Why she wanted to take her own life?"

I paused, and my teeth closed around my bottom lip. I'd only known Emily for two days but, right now, she was my best friend. In for a penny, in for a pound.

I exhaled. "She told me she was pregnant."

Emily's eyes enlarged to the size of gingernut biscuits. "Pregnant? Why didn't you say so?"

"Um, she asked me not to tell anyone. She said, 'none of them must find out'."

"Them? Who's them?" Emily sat back. "Am I one of them?"

"No. I don't think so. I'm sorry; I should've told you before. And I guess now it doesn't matter."

"Poor Josh." Emily frowned. "He would've made a great father. Your news makes me even more sure he didn't kill her. He loves kids. He helps out at Redcliff School for Disabled Children. Whenever the school has an outing, Josh volunteers to go along. All the kids love him."

I tore the piece of paper from the pad and started a new sheet headed 'Josh'.

"Apart from being a gentle, simple, soul, what do we know about Josh?"

"A young lad in his early twenties. He's lived here all his life and worked on his dad's fishing boat since he was a boy. And is right now in police custody, scared out of his wits, and you have information that could clear his name. What are we waiting for?"

"You're right." I stood, grabbed my coat and beanie hat and pushed in my chair. "Are you with me, Emily?"

"Of course." She jumped up, and we headed out of the door.

Redcliff-upon-Sea's police station stood in a side street; a Victorian, stone building with sash windows which reminded me of a scene from a 1960s period drama. We walked up the two stone steps and pushed the door open.

A rosy-cheeked, plump, middle-aged policeman stood behind the counter. "Morning, Miss Emily," he said. "Bit cold and damp outside today, isn't it? Should brighten up later."

I loved his country accent, which reminded me of the farmer on the TV advert for Flora margarine. I also loved that folks in this town knew each other. Not like my old life, where people were only friendly if you could be useful to them.

"Morning, Bert. This is my new friend, Shiraz."

"Shiraz, eh? That's not a name we hear too often. Are you visiting Redcliff for long?"

For some reason it took Bert longer to push his sentences out than policemen I'd met in London.

"I'm not visiting; I've moved here. I'm a member of Redcliff Volunteer Marine Rescue. With Emily."

"Well, isn't that wonderful," said Bert. "Not that I'm used to seeing nice young ladies like you involved in dangerous emergency services work."

"Bert, don't be so old-fashioned," said Emily. "We're here to talk about the events of two nights ago. The girl who died at West Cove."

"Died? Murdered you mean." Bert pushed himself off the counter, held his uniform lapels and tiptoed. "I'll have you know; I was the one who arrested her killer." He pointed over his shoulder with his thumb, leant forward conspiratorially and lowered his voice. "We've got him in custody now."

"Josh Rawlings?" said Emily. "Don't be daft. He's not capable of it."

"That's what I said, when Sarge told me we were going to arrest him. I said, Sarge, I've known young Josh all his life, and his father as well." Bert looked down and sighed. "I'd never have believed he had it in him." He shook his head. "Terrible to see a young lad go bad."

He pursed his lips and frowned. "How did you know it was Josh we'd arrested?"

"Small town," said Emily. "You'll never keep that under wraps."

I stepped forward. "Bert, I mean, Officer. I believe I have information that clears Josh. He's innocent, and I can prove it."

Bert's face took on a serious expression, more like the city police officers I was accustomed to. "Have you now, Miss? If you'd like to wait, please, I'll fetch my sergeant, and we'll take a statement."

He turned and lumbered through a door behind the counter.

I sidled closer to Emily. "They've already made up their minds Josh is guilty. My story of Kateryna being suicidal won't change anything."

"Shh. Let's see what the sergeant says."

Bert bumped the rear door open again, followed by a tall man with crewcut black hair wearing an immaculately pressed uniform. For some reason, I instantly mistrusted him.

Bert stood back while the new man addressed me.

"Morning, Ms...?"

"Jones. Shiraz Jones." I held out my hand. "And this is my friend, Emily Philpot."

It felt odd to be introducing Emily when she'd lived here all her life, and I'd only arrived three days ago, but she didn't seem to know the sergeant.

"Sergeant Will Bishopstone. You mentioned to my constable you were in possession of information regarding an event which occurred on Friday night." He pulled out a pad and pen.

"I am."

"Let's start with your full name, address and phone number."

"Shiraz Jones."

"Shiraz, as in the wine?"

"Like the wine. I'm staying at Melville Cottage, on the seafront. My number's 07700 900119."

"Thank you, Ms Jones. What else d'you have to tell me?"

"Kateryna wasn't murdered. It was suicide."

Sergeant Will looked up and furrowed his eyebrows. "What makes you think it was murder to begin with?"

"I understand you're holding a suspect. Josh Rawlings."

"We may be. Why do you believe that?"

"Your constable confirmed it."

Bert's cheeks turned the colour of Braeburn apples, and he studied his shoes. "Does anyone want a cup of tea?" he asked. "We have chocolate digestives."

"Not now, Bert," said Will, glaring at him. "Make yourself useful and organise the interview notes from earlier."

"Right-o, Sarge." Bert busied himself with a pile of papers.

Sergeant Will returned his gaze to me. "Yes, we are holding Josh. What information d'you have that may assist our investigation?"

I planted both hands on the counter and leant forwards. "I was one of the last, possibly the last person to see her alive."

"That seems unlikely, based on our evidence." He narrowed his eyes. "Unless you murdered her yourself."

A cold shiver ran from my head to my stomach, and I stepped back.

"Don't be ridiculous," said Emily. "Listen to what Shiraz has to say before you jump to any silly conclusions."

"As I was saying," I continued, "I saw Kateryna the day she died. I was in Emily's café enjoying a coffee when Kateryna entered. She sat down, and I asked her if she wanted to talk to me, as she'd obviously been crying."

Sergeant Will scribbled notes furiously. "Had you met her before this occasion?"

"I'd only arrived in town the previous day."

"New in town and, on your first day here, one of our residents dies. How did you know her name?" He folded his arms and challenged me to respond.

"She told me. And then she said she was pregnant. She also told me she wanted to kill herself. Don't you see? It was suicide. Josh had nothing to do with it."

"We'll be the judge of that," said Will.

"It sounds to me like you've already been the judge and jury," said Emily. "And executioner."

Will ignored her. "Then what happened?"

"Then," I said, "Emily brought Kateryna one of her hot chocolates."

Bert looked up from the filing cabinet. "I can vouch that Miss Emily's hot chocolates are particularly delicious. Especially when accompanied by one of her crumbly home-made scones."

"Thank you, Bert," said Will. "The quality of Emily's hot chocolates is not crucial evidence in this investigation."

"What was it you said to me yesterday, Sarge? No clue should be left unconsidered?"

"I do appreciate the reminder. We're all in agreement Emily makes very tasty hot chocolates. Please go on, Ms Jones."

I cleared my throat. "The door swung open, and a man came in to buy something."

"Nigel, from Redcliff Manor," interrupted Emily. "Grantley Bramhall's personal assistant. He buys two pastries every weekday."

"Does he prefer the cheese pastries or the ham ones?" asked Bert. "Or the sweet ones with the gooey, chocolate insides? I'm particularly partial to one of your chocolate pastries for lunch myself."

Will clenched his teeth and turned sideways slowly. "Constable, your preferred lunchtime refreshment is not relevant to this case."

Bert tapped one finger on his lips. "You say he buys two pastries each day? They're very filling. D'you think he eats them both himself? Maybe this is a clue?"

Will leant on the table and covered his face with his hand. He looked up. "Bert, please. Could we allow Ms Jones to continue with her statement? Ms Jones, please go on."

I hid a smile. "Kateryna told me she didn't want this Nigel chap to see her. At that point, I didn't know who he was, so I'd no idea why she needed to hide from him. She concealed her face and suggested, while Nigel had his back to us, we should escape the café and talk while we walked. I agreed, as I wanted to keep her mind from..." My voice tailed off.

Emily laid her hand on my arm. I glanced towards her and smiled.

Will scribbled notes. "Where did you walk to?"

"She led me away from town, along the pebble beach under the cliffs, and began to tell me her story, about how she'd fled Ukraine, left her family behind and started a job at Redcliff Manor. Something about Mrs Bramhall finding it for her. Apparently, Kateryna was good with figures and loved horses, and they needed a bookkeeper and a stable hand, so she was a perfect match."

Will wrote more notes.

"Then, she led me on this steep path, and we arrived at the top of the cliffs."

"The cliffs she was pushed from? Above West Cove?"

"She wasn't pushed. I'm trying to tell you. She explained to me, she wasn't happy at Redcliff Manor. She said nobody there speaks to her unless they're asking her to do something. They don't treat her well."

"I can believe that," said Bert. "A few weeks ago, I had to give Grantley Bramhall a parking ticket, as his Rolls Royce was stationed in the bus stop outside the butcher's. He called me a very rude word. Me, an officer of the law, and he says something like that. I haven't heard anyone use that word since old Tommy Colstead sliced his finger open with a fish gutting knife."

Sergeant Will clenched and unclenched his fists. "Thank you, Bert, for your character summation of Grantley Bramhall. I think we all understand your opinion of his personality."

I continued. "Kateryna sat right on the edge of the cliffs, dangling her feet over. Honestly, I thought she'd end it all there, and I grabbed hold of her to stop her throwing herself off. She didn't appreciate this, and she told me she hated me like all the others. Then she ran away, and that was the last I saw of her. So you see, she must've come back later when I'd gone, and jumped."

I sobbed, and Emily put her arm around my shoulders.

"I'm so sorry," I said. "I tried to save her. She was such a pretty girl, with her whole life ahead of her."

I bawled out loud, and Bert passed me a box of tissues. "There, there, Miss. Shall I make you a cup of tea?"

"Yes, please," I sniffed.

Bert smiled. "And a chocolate digestive?"

"Okay. Thank you." I gave him a half-smile.

Bert disappeared through the rear door, and I heard a kettle boil. I wiped my eyes with a tissue and spread mascara around my face again. Emily squeezed my arm. "Well done," she whispered.

Will closed the pad of notes. "Thank you, Ms Jones. Your account is all very interesting. But there's one thing it doesn't explain."

"Oh? What's that?"

He extracted another sheet of paper from under his pad and held it up. "This is the initial autopsy report. Yes, she fell down the cliff and into the sea. That agrees with your theory. But this tells me she was dead before she hit the water."

CHAPTER SEVEN

"I was so convinced she'd committed suicide," I said, as Emily and I sat at her dining table. Boots lay in the centre partly concealing a pad of paper.

"And I'm sure it wasn't Josh that killed her," said Emily. "But this new sergeant seems to have made up his mind." She grabbed my arm across the table. "We have to get to the bottom of this."

"What d'you mean, we?" I asked. "We're not detectives. You run a café, I'm an ex-social butterfly, and we both volunteer for marine rescue, but we've no experience solving crimes."

"Think back," she said. "Before we walked to the police station. What were we doing?"

"Sitting at my kitchen table, chatting. Just like we are now."

"What else were we doing?"

"I don't know. Drinking tea?"

"We were making lists about people connected with Kateryna's death. It was your idea, remember?"

I frowned. "That doesn't make me a detective."

"It's a start. You were probably the last person to talk to Kateryna. You might've been the only person in the world she told about her pregnancy."

I took a deep breath, and the feeling returned to me of being young and completely alone. My eyes watered, as I knew what Kateryna must have been going through.

"I felt sorry for her, yes. She had no one to turn to."

"I'm more concerned about Josh," said Emily. "Kateryna's gone. We can't bring her back. But we can help him."

"The autopsy said she was dead before she fell into the sea. I don't know how the police know the order of events. Maybe she hit her head after jumping?"

Emily laughed. "A minute ago you weren't a detective; now you're a forensic pathologist."

"Oh. Yes. Okay, let's assume the report's correct, and someone killed her, then pushed her off the cliff. You're sure it wasn't Josh? Whenever there's a murder, the police always accuse the partner before anyone, don't they?"

"They have in this case. I hope he has an alibi. Josh wouldn't have the brains to kill anyone."

"So if Josh didn't kill her, who did?"

Emily smiled and sat back in her chair. "That, Shiraz Jones, ex-social butterfly and marine rescue volunteer, is what you and I are going to find out."

"Really?"

"What if we don't? Kateryna's life's over. Josh's will be as well, if he's found guilty. That poor boy will never stand up to some clever lawyer's cross-examination. He'll end up getting all confused and confessing to something he hasn't done. We have to help him."

"But what if he really did kill her?"

Emily found a pen. "Let's keep going. Did you bring the piece of paper we started making notes on?"

"Yep. In my pocket." I tugged it out and unfolded it, as we heard three sharp raps from the bottom of the stairs.

Emily clumped down and opened her door. I heard Oscar's voice.

"Here's your torch back. Thanks so much."

"Any time, Oscar. D'you want to pop up? I'll put the kettle on."

"Thanks, I'd love a tea. My wife's at a church lunch. Not my scene."

Emily and Oscar appeared at the top of the stairs.

He waved at me. "Afternoon, Shiraz. How's Redcliff Marine Rescue?"

"Hi, Oscar. I haven't completed any training since I saw you yesterday. There's more tomorrow night."

"Take a seat," said Emily. "Would you like a filled roll, either of you? I've some in the fridge that didn't sell yesterday. They need eating." She brought over a plate, and we selected one each.

"So what d'you know, Oscar? What's the inside track about the murder?" Emily called from the kitchen as the kettle boiled.

Oscar sat back in his chair. "The police have their suspect. As far as they're concerned, the case is closed."

"I know," I said, unwrapping my roll, which was stuffed with so much ham and salad I wondered how it would fit in my mouth. "We visited the police station this morning, so I could tell them what Kateryna said about wanting to kill herself. I was convinced it was suicide. But they said the autopsy indicated she died before she plummeted over the cliff."

Emily plopped three mugs on the table and sat with us. "Shiraz and I are going to get to the bottom of this." She smiled and nodded at me. "Aren't we?"

"Um, I suppose so. We're not exactly qualified or experienced. But a girl's lost her life, and there's about to be a miscarriage of justice. Would you help us, Oscar?"

Oscar steepled his fingers. "Twenty years ago, I was the policeman here. The only policeman. Now there are three police officers in Redcliff, and all of them put together couldn't solve a crime using good, old-fashioned detective work. Constable Bert's too nice a chap; he takes everyone at face value. It's about time he retired. Constable Lachlan's fresh out of police college. Nineteen years old, and he thinks he knows everything. Just because he can work a computer doesn't make him an expert. And this new sergeant; I don't know his background. Something's not right about him. Where has he come from, all smart and ambitious, to wind up somewhere like little old Redcliff-upon-Sea, and why?"

"We met Bert and the sergeant this morning," I said. "His name's Will. We didn't see Constable Lachlan. I gave them my statement, but they weren't very interested."

"What've you come up with so far?"

"Kateryna was from Ukraine. She had one brother who was killed in the war and one who's fighting. Her parents wanted her to flee the country."

"Very sensible," said Oscar. "How did she end up here?"

"The lady who owns Redcliff Manor's involved with a charity that resettles refugees. She needed a bookkeeper, and Kateryna had studied accounting, so she employed her." I paused and took a bite of roll. "And she knew something about horses, so she looked after the stables too."

"Who could've wanted her dead?" Oscar rubbed his hands together enthusiastically. "Make a list of everyone, no matter how unlikely."

I smoothed out the paper which I'd written on that morning. "Number one is herself. She wanted to die. She told me."

"But the autopsy disagrees with the suicide theory."

"How do they know that?"

"It's only possible to drown when you're breathing," said Oscar. "You can't drown after you're dead. And she didn't die by drowning. Cause of death was head trauma from a blunt object."

"Have you seen the autopsy?"

Oscar gave a slight smile. "I can't confirm or deny if I have. Keep going. Next suspect."

"Josh. Josh is the most obvious person to have murdered her, simply because he was her boyfriend. Nothing else points to his guilt, apart from that."

"Nothing else that we know. I haven't heard if he's given a valid alibi. So let's look at it from the point of view that he did do it. Play it out. Kateryna and him were walking along the cliffs."

"She told me it was her favourite place to sit and watch the gulls."

"Right. They'd gone there together to watch the gulls, they had a quarrel, he bashed her over the head with a rock and pushed her over the edge."

Emily shook her head slowly. "Oscar, you've known Josh all his life. And his dad. D'you believe that happened?"

"I don't. But let's keep an open mind for now. Who else could've had a motive to kill Kateryna? Who else did she know in the town? What about the people living at the manor?"

"Emily, d'you have any more paper?"

She tugged the pad from under Boots. I giggled as he slid along the table with it, then swatted her hand before relinquishing his resting spot.

"Kateryna mentioned four people at the manor," I said. "First, Grantley Bramhall. What do we know about him?"

"He has unlimited money," said Oscar. "A Rolls Royce, an apartment in the poshest London neighbourhood, Redcliff Manor, which he's had refurbished to a very high standard; no expense spared. I'm told his wine cellar has ten thousand bottles."

"Okay. I get the picture. Mr Moneybags. Would he have any reason to kill his stable hand?"

"I've got it," said Emily. "Grantley Bramhall found Kateryna was mistreating his horses, he bashed her over the head with a horseshoe in his anger, panicked when he realised what he'd done, dragged her body to the cliffs and threw it over to make it look like an accident." She gave us two thumbs-up. "Case closed."

I shook my head. "Emily, that's very unlikely. It's perfectly possible Grantley Bramhall could've bashed her over the head with a horseshoe, but Redcliff Manor's at the top of the town. It must be two miles from the sea. That's a long way to drag a dead body."

"Write it down," said Oscar. "At this point in our investigation, we mustn't close any doors. Who else did Kateryna mention?"

"There's Nigel. The man who calls into Emily's café to buy pastries."

Emily frowned. "I can't see him being physically capable of killing a young, fit adult. He's a wet whistle. A scrawny weakling. I know I could fight him off, and I'm not exactly tall, so I'm sure Kateryna could have."

"Any motive?" asked Oscar.

"Again, who knows? We don't have any information about him. All we know is he's Grantley Bramhall's personal assistant and chauffeur. Anything could've happened between him and Kateryna."

"Okay, park that thought for now. Who else?"

"Charlie Bramhall." I held up one finger. "He must be a similar age to Kateryna."

"The son?" asked Oscar. "We hardly ever see him here. He lives in London, and swans in and out in his red, convertible, sports car. I'd be surprised if he and Kateryna had anything to do with each other."

I made a note: need to investigate further.

"That's four potential suspects," said Emily, "including Josh. Anyone else?"

I nodded. "Kateryna told me there were two staff members at the house. Nigel's one of them. Who's the other?"

"Joan Kilpatrick," said Oscar. "The housekeeper. She's been there for ever. She nursed the woman who used to live at the manor until she sold up, and Grantley bought the house. Gosh. I'd almost forgotten about her. I haven't seen her for years."

"Would she have any motive for murder?"

"I can't imagine so. She must be over eighty."

"Maybe Kateryna discovered some deep, dark secret about her past?" said Emily. "Perhaps Joan had blackmailed the old lady, and Kateryna found out about this? Then Joan murdered her to cover her tracks. Case closed."

Oscar shook his head. "Very far-fetched. And how would an eighty-year-old woman have thrown Kateryna's body over the cliff?"

"You told us to keep an open mind."

"We don't have enough information about these people at the house," I said, running my eyes up and down the writing pad. "We'll never work out who murdered her."

Oscar clasped his hands together and leant on his elbows. "If you don't have the information which you need to solve the crime, you'll have to obtain it."

"That's easy for you to say, Oscar; you're an ex-policeman. Where would we get it from?"

"Four of your suspects are in the same location. Maybe you should pay Redcliff Manor a visit?"

Emily puffed. "What, walk up the drive and say, 'Hello, we're Emily and Shiraz, marine rescue volunteers, and we're here to interview you about your whereabouts on the night in question.' I don't think so."

I leant forward. "Oscar's right. We need to become intimate with the four occupants. And I know how we'll go about it."

CHAPTER EIGHT

Murph was in full form at Monday's marine rescue training following a victory over his laptop. I sat with Emily and three other new recruits watching his presentation about the names of various parts of the vessel, and I tried to write notes as fast as my pen would scribble. At one point, Boots decided the presentation was too boring for his tastes, and he leapt on the keyboard, then scrabbled and clawed as Murph lifted him up and plopped him on the ground.

Murph continued explaining marine terms and phrases. The thought of whipping through the waves with the salt spray on my face made me lean forward and grab the edges of the seat, and when Murph concluded by mentioning we'd crew the rescue boat for the first time at the weekend, a combination of nerves and elation washed through me.

This is what I came here to do. One day, I want to be like Murph. Standing at the helm of the rescue vessel, saving people from drowning and teaching others to follow in my footsteps.

I nudged Emily as we stood up.

"Shall we ask him?"

"Now?"

"No time like the present."

I approached Murph, and Emily hung a step behind me.

"Shiraz and Emily," he said. "My star female pupils. What can I do for you? Did you have a question?"

"Yes, but not about anything you've taught tonight."

"I'm not sure I follow you."

"Do we ever do fundraising? Standing on the street rattling cans, asking people for donations?"

"Ye-es. During Marine Rescue week, in summer each year. And at our annual barn dance, held shortly before Christmas. We receive no government funding; we're completely reliant on public generosity."

"Do we ever fundraise in midwinter? Like, now?"

"With no tourists in town, it's hardly worth it. Why?"

"Emily and I were thinking of taking a collection tin to the High Street and seeing if anyone gives us a few coins."

Murph stood. "Baffling bobstays. You are keen recruits. Your timing's good, to be honest. The bank account's low, and we've several bills due this month: insurance, boat engine servicing and electricity; they've all come at once this year. We could use any funds we can get."

"Great. Where do we find a tin?"

"I'll grab one from the storage cupboard. There are some shaped like our rescue vessel. Although I don't think you'll get many donations. Not at this time of year."

Murph opened a door at the rear of the training room, and we headed into the boat shed where the rescue vessel stood on its trailer, ready for active service. While Murph and Emily rummaged through a cupboard, I ran my hand along the side of the bright-red boat. I patted it, and the metal responded with a dull thunk.

One day, I'll drive you. And I'll be a rescue hero. Not someone else's sidekick.

Emily returned carrying a miniature boat model. She passed it to me, and I observed the slot in the top for donors to poke money into.

"Thanks, Murph," I said. "We'll bring it back brimming with coins and notes."

"I do hope so. Good luck. See you Sunday for on-water training. It'll be the three of us, plus a qualified crewman."

We stood outside the marine rescue station in the dark of a winter's evening. Boots followed us and smooched around Emily's legs.

"Have you been sleeping in the boat again? Careful; you'll take a trip to sea accidentally." She bent down to stroke him. "Are you hungry? Let's find you some food."

She held the boat-shaped collection box up at me. "What, exactly, are you proposing to do with this?"

"This miniature boat is our ticket into Redcliff Manor."

"It is?"

"Yep. I'll find you after the café closes tomorrow. We, Emily, are going on an adventure."

"We're going to walk up the driveway of Redcliff Manor, bold as brass, and ask for a donation?"

Emily jogged to catch up with me, as I marched up the High Street with our collecting tin.

"Of course. Everyone says Grantley Bramhall's got oodles of money, so we'll ask for some. And while we're there, we'll have a look around."

"What if he says no? What if he won't let us in? What if... what if he's the murderer, and he kills us too?"

I paused, turned and faced her. "How are we going to find out the answers to those questions, Emily, by sitting at your kitchen table and writing lists on paper?"

"You really are getting into this detective thing, aren't you?"

"A young woman's been killed. We don't know how pregnant she was. She's lived here for six months, so she could've almost been in her third trimester."

"She might've been pregnant when she arrived here. Maybe she had a boyfriend back in Ukraine?"

"Now you're starting to think like Sherlock Holmes, Emily. You're right. We can't rule anything out."

"Yes," said Emily, warming to her subject, "Her old boyfriend in Ukraine knew she was pregnant, didn't want her to have the baby, so he tracked her down to Redcliff-upon-Sea, bashed her with a rock and threw her over the cliff. Case closed. We don't need to go to Redcliff Manor anymore." She right wheeled and walked back the other way.

"Don't be silly." I grabbed her arm and tugged her up the High Street. "For starters, how would any boyfriend in Ukraine know she was pregnant? She didn't look pregnant when I saw her. I mean, if she hadn't had a winter's coat on, her bump might've been obvious. But regardless, when she left Ukraine, she would've been a few weeks pregnant at most."

"But it still could've been someone from Ukraine that killed her? An old contact of some kind?"

"As Oscar said, don't rule anything out. We'll add 'mysterious unknown assassin from Ukraine' to our list of suspects when we return."

I marched on. "And then there's Josh. You're convinced he's innocent. From what I've learnt, he's a gentle lad who wouldn't hurt a fly and is quaking in his boots in police custody. We can't allow this crime to be pinned on the wrong person." I stopped at the point where the buildings ended, and the country road curved away from the town. "That's something we could ask Oscar. How long can the police hold Josh for?"

"It's either 24 or 48 hours," said Emily. "I read it in a crime novel."

"If it's 24 hours, he'll have been released by now. After we've visited the manor, we could pop into the police station and ask if he's still being held for questioning. And if he's not, we'll find him and ask some questions of our own."

We walked further up the road. Grey clouds scudded across the sky and threatened rain. The wind whistled through the bare, winter trees, and dead leaves and twigs blew across the lane. The fields, which in a few months would be filled with the shoots of new growth, were dark brown with freshly ploughed soil.

It was a very dull, grey kind of day.

As we reached the old, rusty signpost which pointed the way to Redcliff Manor, something shot out of the side turning which definitely wasn't dull or grey.

We pressed ourselves against the hedgerow as a red sports car skidded from the lane, swerved left without pausing and accelerated up the road away from town.

Emily and I looked at each other wide-eyed.

"Charlie Bramhall?" I said.

"I guess so. Not too many red Ferraris in Redcliff."

"That's one suspect we won't be able to interview today, then."

"The way he's driving, we might never interview him. He's going to get himself killed."

"Or kill someone else."

"Or maybe," said Emily, "he's already done that? Perhaps that's what happened. Charlie Bramhall killed Kateryna in a car accident, didn't want anyone to find out, so he threw her body over the cliff. Case closed."

"Did you see any damage on his car? Dear me, Emily, your theories are becoming less and less likely."

We strolled along the lane towards Redcliff Manor. High hedges hemmed us in on both sides. At one point, we nipped into a farm gateway as we heard the sound of an approaching engine, before realising it was a tractor working in a nearby field.

We rounded a bend in the lane to find black, wrought-iron gates blocking our way. I held their bars like a prisoner and peered along the gravel drive visible on the other side. Through trees, I spied the outline of a large, red-brick building. I reckoned the drive looped around in front of it.

"This place is so grand," said Emily. "I came here once as a little girl. I know it must've been very dilapidated then, because I needed a wee-wee, and my mother asked the lady who lived here where the toilet was. She suggested it might be nicer if I peed in the garden."

I giggled. "Emily, is that really true?"

"Yes. Fortunately, we were alone, so no one could watch me watering the herbaceous border."

"We're alone now, and the only way I can see for us to get in, is to press this intercom." I pushed a button below a circular glass aperture, which I was certain contained a camera.

WOOF

WOOF WOOF WOOF WOOF WOOF WOOF WOOF

I released my hold on the gate. "Uh-oh. How many are there?"

"At least three, and they're coming this way."

CHAPTER NINE

Three Doberman dogs stuck their noses through gaps in the gates and barked enthusiastically.

"Help!" I shouted. "I hope the gates don't swing open automatically. We'll be eaten."

"Is it Dobermans or Dobermen?"

"What?"

"The plural of Doberman."

"We're inches from the slavering jaws of dogs almost as large as us, and you're worried about grammar?"

A speaker crackled next to the buzzer.

"Yes?" said a male voice.

"Um, hi." I leant my head forward and simultaneously tried to keep every part of my body out of canine tasting distance. "We're from Redcliff Marine Rescue. We're collecting money for, um, charity."

CLICK.

I turned to Emily and yelled above the woofs. "D'you think they heard me?"

"No idea." Her voice seemed too loud as the dogs ceased barking, turned tail and sprinted away from the gates, which slowly opened by themselves.

We hid behind the gatepost, as if it would protect us from woman-eating Dobermans. Or Dobermen. "Are those dogs going to reappear?" asked Emily. "There's nothing between us and them now."

I held my breath as the gates fully opened, and the gap between them became wide enough for a vehicle.

"Come on." I stepped forward.

"What, in there with the dogs?"

"Yes, in here with the dogs. How are we going to gather any information if we stand outside like a couple of chickens? Follow me."

We edged up the drive, keeping careful eyes and ears out for the Dobermans. As the drive looped around, a four-storey, box-shaped house came fully into view. Two vast, grey-framed sash windows stood either side of a tall, burgundy front door which proudly displayed a central, brass knob. A single-storey outbuilding stood to the right of the main house, built in the same style, but clearly a modern addition. An open garage door revealed the bonnet of a sparkling Rolls Royce. A second garage beside it was empty.

I noticed openings to cellars under the house, and dormer windows indicated it had attics above. The black wrought-iron fence surrounded the entire front garden. Lion statues mounted on pillars guarded both sides of five wide, stone steps leading up to the entrance.

"Rampant," I said, under my breath.

"What was that?" asked Emily.

I turned to her. "The lions. That pose is known as rampant. Standing on their hind feet erect with one paw clawing the air. My father was an architect. He knew about classical buildings."

"They're scary," said Emily. "I wouldn't want to visit after dark."

As we approached, a distant slit of choppy sea became visible across meadows to our left. I narrowed my eyes and peered at a thin, winding path that led past tall, broad trees. The track originated from the rear of the house, behind a high stone wall with a white, wooden gate.

I realised this must've been Kateryna's route to her favourite place to sit and watch the gulls.

The front door swung open, and a slight, thin man dressed in a jumper and slacks stood framed in the doorway. Probably aged in his late forties, but wearing clothes that would've suited a man thirty years older, he appeared remarkably tiny for the entrance, and I had a brief giggle to myself as I wondered if he struggled to reach the doorknob.

The man from the café. Nigel. Grantley Bramhall's chauffeur and assistant.

We stopped two steps below him.

I thrust the money box in his direction. "We're collecting for Redcliff Marine Rescue and hoped you might be able to offer a donation. Our organisation saves lives at sea and we receive no government funding; we're completely reliant on public generosity."

Phew, I think that's what Murph taught me word for word.

"Here." He wiggled his hand in his pocket, tugged something out and leant towards me. I held the plastic boat-shaped box up and heard a single coin CLUNK in the bottom.

He sneered. "Was mine your first donation?"

"Um, yes. We decided to start at the top of the town and work down the hill."

A rich, deep voice sounded from inside the house. "Who is it, Nigel?"

"Two young ladies collecting for charity, Mr Bramhall. I'll send them on their way."

"Two young ladies, eh?" said the voice. "How delightful. Don't keep them waiting. Invite them in."

Nigel stepped back against the wide front door, gestured with his left arm and we ascended the remaining two steps into the lion's den.

The rampant lion's den.

"Wait here," commanded Nigel. He entered a side room and closed the door. We stood inside the cavernous, square entrance hall. The floor was checkerboarded in black-and-white, marble, diamond-shaped tiles, each around two feet across. A crystal chandelier hung above the centre and, against the far wall, I observed an oversized, grey, stone fireplace, although no fire burnt in it today.

To its left, a blackened coal scuttle, empty of fuel. To the right of the fireplace, solid brass implements hung from a stand: tongs, a brush and a dustpan. A gap showed where a fourth implement should've been, and I racked my brains to think what was missing. The mantelpiece displayed a pair of statues, one at each end, and a gong on a stand in the centre. But it was what hung above the fireplace that drew my eye. As a girl, I'd visited stately homes with my parents. My father the architect, and my mother the interior designer.

I'd never seen anything like this in a country house.

I passed Emily the collecting box to hold and took two steps towards the larger-than-life-size painting.

Emily followed. "Who d'you think she is?" she asked.

"No idea, but she has such a voluptuous body. Luxurious hair, too. I love the pose, lying naked on her back on the four-poster bed, with her head dangling over the edge, and her hair almost touching the floor. I'd be flattered if someone painted me like that."

Emily made a face. "Ugh. There's no way anyone would hang a nude picture of me on their wall. I'd be far too embarrassed to allow it."

I stepped forward, my head tilted to one side, touching my shoulder. "I want to turn the painting upside down so I can see her face."

"Stunning, isn't she?" The male voice we'd heard earlier echoed around the hall, and we turned to find a tall, middle-aged man dressed in an outfit as if he were about to march into the countryside and shoot pheasants. He wore a tweed jacket, fawn-coloured trousers and a flat cap. A light-blue shirt and red-and-blue diagonally striped tie completed the ensemble.

He planted his hands on his hips and appraised us as if we were offerings in a cattle market. "What have we here?" He raised one eyebrow. "Aren't you two a fine pair of fillies?"

"I beg your pardon." I took a step towards him. "I don't know who you think you're talking to, but we're marine rescue volunteers, collecting for our charity. We save lives at sea. We're not 'a fine pair of fillies'."

The man patted the air with both hands. "Calm down, calm down. I'm Grantley Bramhall, squire of Redcliff Manor, local benefactor and all-round jolly good chap. Were you admiring my painting?"

"Um, yes. She's certainly a striking subject. Where did you buy it?"

"Buy it? I commissioned it. It's my wife, in her younger years."

"Your wife?"

"Yes. Not that I've seen her looking like that for decades. In fact, I haven't seen her at all recently. Hmph. Fickle woman. She lives in our London apartment and spends her time lunching and working for charity."

He paused, then boomed at us again. "Do either of you know anything about horses?"

"Horses?" I glanced at Emily.

Her lips formed a straight line, and she shook her head once. "Sorry, we've no experience with horses."

"Pity," said Grantley. "I need a new stable hand. The last one's not with us anymore."

Ah-ha. This could be the first clue. Play dumb.

"Not with you anymore? Did she resign?"

"No. The silly girl went and got herself killed by her idiot boyfriend. I'd warned her about him. Wouldn't permit him on my property. No idea what these working-class types are capable of."

"Killed? How awful."

"Pfff. Fortunately, the police arrested him as soon as I provided the evidence."

"Evidence? What evidence?"

"The fact they'd been dating, of course. What other evidence is needed? No one apart from him knew her in Redcliff. I don't think she'd met anyone outside the manor."

"She came into my café once a week," said Emily. "Every Saturday..."

I silently shushed her and made a subtle zipping motion across my lips. I wanted Grantley to give us the information, not her.

"...but I didn't know her," she finished.

"Saturday's Nigel's day off." Grantley pointed at the closed door where the chauffeur had shut himself. "Nigel, my personal assistant, walks down to the café each day to collect the pastries. I must say"—he placed both hands on his stomach—"they're delicious. Especially the yummy chocolate-filled ones. D'you make them yourself?"

Emily folded her arms. "Everything in my café's home-made."

Grantley tiptoed and peered behind her. "You don't have any with you now, d'you?"

This conversation needs to get back on track.

"Mr Bramhall, how long had your stable girl been seeing this local boy?"

"Months. I caught him on the premises back in the autumn and chased him out myself. With a shotgun."

My eyebrows raised. "A shotgun? Were you going to shoot him?"

"Of course not. It was the first day of the shooting season, so my guns needed a clean. I wanted to frighten him off, and it worked. But I knew they were still seeing each other. She used to sneak him in and out of the side gate. Mrs Kilpatrick, the housekeeper, watched them from an upstairs window, hugging each other goodnight. I told the stable girl to keep him away. The last thing I wanted was for any of my antiques to go missing. But she didn't heed my warnings, and now she's dead. I need to find a new stable hand and a new bookkeeper. I don't suppose any of your friends fit the bill? It's dreadfully inconvenient."

I puffed at his callousness. "I'd say it's dreadfully inconvenient for the girl who died."

Grantley's attitude suddenly changed, and he seemed to remember why we were here.

"I donated a large sum to your organisation by bank transfer last month as a Christmas present. I remember, I gave a similar sum to the police benevolent fund at the same time."

"Oh. Um, thank you."

He opened the huge front door. "See yourselves out. And don't forget, if you know anyone looking for a job, send them my way."

He swivelled on one heel and marched back into the room he'd come from, closing the door behind him.

Emily turned to me. "What a pompous idiot."

"Shh," I lowered my voice. "Do you realise something?"

"What?" she whispered.

"We've just spoken to two of the primary suspects."

"Woah. I never thought of that. We could've been in conversation with a killer. That's scary and exciting all at once."

"I know. And we're standing in the hallway of the house Kateryna lived in, and no one's watching us."

"Uh-oh. What are you thinking of?"

"Having a quick look around. This might be our best chance. Come on."

A corridor led off the hall to the rear of the house. We tiptoed along it and peeked into open doors: a laundry, a store and a toilet. The end of the corridor opened into a large country kitchen, immaculately refurbished. White cabinets lined the walls, topped with light-coloured, wooden counters. A pitch-black, cast-iron stove protruded above the work surface.

In the centre, the theme continued with an island breakfast bar and an oval food preparation area. Solid-looking, top-quality metal utensils dangled from a rack fixed to the ceiling.

Emily's jaw dropped. "Wow. I wish I had a kitchen like this in the café. I barely have room to turn around." She placed the collecting box on the worktop and ran her fingers over the stove.

"Can you see any clues?"

"What, exactly, are we supposed to be looking for?"

"I don't know. A murder weapon, or something to indicate who might've killed Kateryna."

"Right. Like a murderer's going to leave a cricket bat lying around with a museum label on it saying, 'Blunt object. As used in the death of a young woman'."

"Shh. Look out of the window. What can you see?"

"Stables? Maybe it's where the horses live?"

The kitchen looked onto a rear yard paved in flagstones. On the opposite side, a whitewashed, stone building which didn't appear to have been included in the recent refurbishment contained three wooden swing doors, each of which had a nameplate and a horseshoe above it. One horseshoe was missing. On the top floor, two small, attic windows looked back into the yard.

Emily glanced over her shoulder towards the front door, and I tugged her arm.

"We know Kateryna worked with the horses. Let's check the stables for clues." I lifted the latch of a rear door, swung it open, and we edged down the two steps. Nobody was around, so we clicked it closed behind us and sidled around the wall at the left-hand edge of the yard. Halfway between the kitchen and the stables, we came across the white, wooden door I'd spotted earlier.

"This is the side door Grantley spoke about." I wiggled the handle. "The shortcut to the meadows and the cliffs, where Grantley Bramhall said Mrs Kilpatrick saw Josh and Kateryna hugging. We'll take a look, after we've checked out the stables."

I pushed a door in the end of the stable building and entered. The smell of horses took me back to my childhood, when I'd had a brief equine interest, and my mother had enrolled me at a local pony club. My enthusiasm had been short-lived after I realised I wasn't going to be cantering through the fields like Black Beauty and caring for horses was a lot of hard work.

Three nags stood in stalls along the right-hand side of the stable, their floor covered in hay. Emily patted the nose of the first brown one, which whinnied and tossed its head up.

"Shh." I placed one upright finger on my lips.

"It wasn't me," said Emily. "It was the horse."

We scuttled past the three animals to the end of the stable and found a rough, wooden stairway which led to an area above. I placed my foot on the first stair.

"What are you doing?" hissed Emily. "We're not supposed to be in here. We need to leave."

"I have a theory," I said, "and I want to check it out." Before she could stop me, I'd climbed the staircase, and she had no choice but to follow.

At the top of the stairs, we found ourselves in a simple room with bare floorboards. The walls were the same whitewashed stone as the exterior, and the two windows we'd seen from the kitchen gave the only light. Four pieces of furniture stood on the floor: a bed, the covers of which were thrown back as if someone had just got up, a double-doored wardrobe, a small, wooden table and a single chair.

96

In the corner, a fitted unit was mounted to the wall containing a sink, a mirror and a small fridge.

"We can't linger here," said Emily. "Whoever's bedroom this is might come back."

"I know whose bedroom this is," I said. "Or was." I plucked a book from the table in a foreign script. "I'll bet this language is Ukrainian. This must've been Kateryna's accommodation. Let's see what else we can find."

I peeked in the mirror, adjusted my hair, then opened the fridge. A half-full bottle of milk rested in the door and, on one shelf, I found an open, plastic container with leftover cooked chicken.

"Nothing to help us in here." I closed the fridge.

Emily winced as a floorboard creaked while I crossed the room and opened the wardrobe.

"We won't find out who murdered her by checking out her fashion sense," said Emily. "And don't ask me to look in the closet. There might be spiders."

"Anything could be a clue." I began to push the clothes left and right. Kateryna hadn't owned many garments; a green jacket smelling of horse, a few tops, two pairs of trousers and a pair of stout shoes.

As I reached the end of the rack of hanging clothes, I found something I hadn't seen since my old life in London.

CHAPTER TEN

I felt the material hanging at the right-hand end of the wardrobe's rail, opened my eyes wide, and turned to Emily.

"Emily, Kateryna owned a Vivienne Westwood dress. Look." I draped the silvery, off-white, glittering gown over my arm and held it away from the hanger.

"Oh my goodness, that is soooo beautiful," said Emily. "I've never seen anything like it." She stroked the fabric.

"D'you know how much these things cost?"

"No idea. A few hundred pounds?"

"Thousands. Maybe tens of thousands. This one looks bespoke." I let the dress drape from the hanger. "Why on earth would a girl who's fled war in Ukraine, and is working as a stable hand and bookkeeper at a country house own a one-off Vivienne Westwood dress?"

"I couldn't guess," said Emily. "Maybe she brought it from Ukraine?"

"I doubt it. She told me she came from a poor background. It's not like she was one of the country's ruling elite." I removed the dress from the hanger and laid it on the bed. A fairytale princess would've been happy to wear it to dance with Prince Charming. As I bent over to smooth it out, my feet banged against something hard.

I knelt on the floor, reached under the bed and slid out a white, paper, rope-handled carrier bag. The logo on the side said, 'Jimmy Choo'. A sturdy, white box was concealed inside. I lifted it out, placed it on the floorboards, and Emily knelt with me. Opening the box revealed bright-pink, stiletto shoes with thin, leather straps and a diamond heart where the toes would poke out.

I inhaled sharply. "These would've cost thousands too."

We drank in the beauty of the shoes for a minute. I imagined them on my own feet. A clattering noise sounded from downstairs.

"Someone's coming," said Emily. She glanced around the room. "Hide in the wardrobe. I'll crawl under the bed. Unless there are spiders."

I held my finger to my lips. "It was a horse. No-one's there."

"We'd better put these back," said Emily. "We're not going to solve the puzzle by looking at them."

"Okay." I re-boxed the shoes and pushed them under the bed.

As I hung the dress back in the wardrobe, I noticed the hanging clothes concealed a two-drawer chest.

The top drawer contained perfectly ordinary underwear.

"No designer clothes in here," I said.

The lower drawer was overstuffed with various socks and stockings. I rummaged amongst them and was about to close it when I noticed a maroon-coloured container peeping through.

I pushed the clothes aside, reached in and tugged out a rectangular jewellery box. It clicked open to reveal a necklace with several large diamonds in a star arrangement.

Emily gasped. "Are those real?"

"I'd say so. This must be worth an absolute fortune." I turned to Emily. "I don't get it. Something's not right here. Kateryna's a refugee from a poor background, she didn't know anyone in town apart from a fisherman she'd hooked up with, she lived in accommodation above her stable hand job, which, frankly, didn't look like it'd pay well, yet she owned a Vivienne Westwood dress, Jimmy Choo shoes and a diamond necklace." I replaced the necklace in its box under the socks.

"D'you think she stole them?" asked Emily.

I shrugged. "Maybe."

"Or Josh stole them for her. He took the train to London, broke into various stores in the luxury shopping streets, stole these items and returned to impress her with them."

"Oh, for goodness' sake. Your conspiracy theories get wilder and wilder. You told me Josh had barely been outside Redcliff-upon-Sea. Let's see if there are any more clues."

A shuffle through papers on Kateryna's table produced handwritten letters in the same language as the book, which I guessed were from her parents in Ukraine, three volumes also in Ukrainian which seemed to be study books about accounting and a *Red Carpet Superstars* magazine.

I picked it up and showed Emily the front page, which featured a photo of a blonde in her thirties draped over the arm of a tuxedo-clad sexagenarian.

"I know her," I said. "Victoria Harrington. Restaurant critic and posh food influencer. Married to Richard Harrington, the man in the suit."

In fact, that picture could've been me. In my old life.

"She looks like a stuck-up cow," said Emily. "And he's old enough to be her father."

She took the magazine and riffled through it. "There are more pictures of them inside. All these people look like they'd stab anyone in the back on their way up the social ladder."

"I used to feature in this magazine," I said. "Alongside my ex-husband. After we, um, parted ways, I didn't want to be that person anymore."

Emily smiled and replaced the magazine on the table. "You're too nice to stab anyone in the back. I can't imagine you being part of that scene."

"I don't think my heart was ever in it."

A floorboard creaked as I changed position. "Shall we leave? The longer we're here, the more likely someone will find us."

We crept down the first few stairs, and I ducked my head under the stable ceiling to check if anyone had entered. The horses continued their afternoon naps, standing on three legs with their fourth one bent slightly at the ankle.

We crept past them to the exit leading to the yard.

"Open it slowly," said Emily. "In case anyone's out there."

I lifted the latch, opened the door a crack and peeked out.

Standing in the yard looking straight back at me was a grinning Doberman.

CHAPTER ELEVEN

I slammed the door and turned around. "Emily. The dogs are out. In the yard. At least one of them is."

"Now what do we do? We're trapped in here with the horses."

"We need to distract them. But how?"

Emily picked up a scoop of pellets. "We could throw them horse food?"

"They won't care about that. They're not vegetarian."

I stood backed against the door with my heart thumpety-thumpetying inside my chest. "I know. The chicken."

"What chicken?"

"In Kateryna's fridge. There was leftover chicken. Grab that; we'll throw it to the dogs and make a run for it out of the side gate."

Emily dashed upstairs two at a time and returned with the plastic dish of chicken. I opened the door slightly, squeezed my eyes shut and threw it into the yard as far as I could.

"Are you ready?" I asked Emily. "That side gate better be unlocked."

She nodded, and I peered out. In the yard, the dog hoovered up the meat. We had two seconds to make our escape.

I flung the door open, and we ran for the gate.

"Emily, it's not opening."

"Shove it."

"I am shoving it."

The dog licked its lips and sniffed the ground looking for more chicken.

We both leant on the gate, gave an adrenaline-fuelled thrust and, as it swung open, we fell into the meadow.

"Run," I yelled, as the noise of barking from the other side of the gate echoed around the yard. "Someone's bound to wonder what the dog's woofing at."

Emily and I sprinted. We paused at a gigantic, gnarled old tree in the middle of the field, halfway between Redcliff Manor and the cliff edge. One of its elderly trunks had long since given up the battle to grow vertically and lay on the ground, forming a convenient seat. Long grass grew underneath it where whoever mowed the meadow couldn't reach.

I plopped on the tree limb, folded my hands on my knees, rested my forehead on my arms and panted.

Emily splayed flat on her back in the grass. "We're...*puff*...going to...*puff*...have to be...*puff*...fitter than this, for marine rescue duty."

"Tell me about it," I said. "Even though it's cold, I'm sweating."

We spent a minute catching our breath. I stole glances around the tree towards the manor to see if anyone had pursued us, but the side gate remained closed.

"Shuffle up," said Emily, standing and brushing grass from her back. "My coat's getting wet." She perched on the tree next to me.

"Recap," I said. "What did we achieve?"

"I ran about a mile. That's a major achievement."

"I meant in the manor. We met two people from our list of potential suspects."

"And we saw a third."

"D'you mean Charlie Bramhall? We barely saw him. All we can deduce from that encounter is that he owns a very nice car and drives it like a lunatic. What did we learn about Nigel?"

"Not much we didn't know already. He's a little, shrew-faced man who works for Grantley Bramhall. I could've told you that without going to the manor."

"We did learn something else. He's tight-fisted. He only gave us one coin for our charity collection."

"I can't see how that could be of any use to our investigation."

"Remember—anything could be a clue. Have we gathered anything about Grantley Bramhall?"

"He's a misogynistic pig. Did you see the way he leered at us? Undressing us with his eyes. I'll bet he wishes he had nude paintings of us to go above the fireplace alongside the one of his wife."

"And," I said, "he was more concerned about finding a new stable hand and bookkeeper than Kateryna's death. Most uncaring."

"He set up Josh, too. With the flimsiest of evidence, he used his status as the local plutocrat to persuade the police to arrest the poor boy. I wish I could remember if it's 24 or 48 hours they're allowed to hold him without charge."

"Let's ask Oscar. Anything else about Grantley?"

"He owns a gun. And he enjoys my home-made pastries. It's nice to know someone appreciates all the effort I go to, rolling the dough, creating the fillings, baking the..."

"Emily, the quality of your cooking is not in dispute here. Grantley Bramhall's appreciation of your café's fare is not relevant to Kateryna's murder."

"You said anything could be a clue."

"I'm sure your pastries are delicious, Emily, but it seems far-fetched anyone would commit murder over a failure to purchase the right ones." I ran a hand through my hair. "That's Grantley Bramhall. Now, what did we learn from our little excursion into Kateryna's apartment? I think that created more questions than answers."

"Correct," said Emily. "The beautiful dress, the am-aaaa-zing shoes and that darling diamond necklace. Where did she get those from, and what possible occasion could she wear them at? Even at the Marine Rescue Christmas Barn Dance no one dresses like that. We all wear our best clothes, but if someone walked in wearing that outfit, the music would stop, and everyone's jaws would hit the ground."

"From what I saw of Kateryna behind the tears and smudged makeup, she was a pretty girl. She'd have pulled off wearing those clothes no problem. Although, that dress was very figure-hugging. She wouldn't have been able to hide her pregnancy under it, like she did with her winter coat. Anything else we learnt?"

"We learnt it's very lucky she had some leftover chicken."

"Um, yes. Although I do hope the Doberman hasn't swallowed an important clue."

We dissolved into giggles at the thought of this, and I again struggled to remember any time when I'd laughed like this with my so-called city friends. This new life of mine was working out really well.

I wiped my eyes. "We're missing something. Something else in Kateryna's apartment. Not the dress, or the shoes or the necklace."

"Or the chicken."

I giggled again. "Nor the chicken. What else was in the fridge? Half a bottle of milk. I'm sure that's not going to help."

"The only other possessions she had were the letters from Ukraine, the accountancy study books and the magazine. Unless you count the underwear and socks." She looked up and shivered. "I'm cold, Shiraz. Could we go home now?"

The late evening sun shone red on the cliffs. I paused at the top of the path and recalled the last time I'd been there, chasing Kateryna, desperate to persuade her not to jump off. And now, the evidence suggested she'd been murdered by persons unknown. If someone had told me a week ago I'd be snooping around stately homes on the trail of a killer, I'd have thought they were nuts.

We scrambled down the path, pushing damp bushes aside, taking care not to trip on tree roots. On the pebble beach at the bottom, we came across Oscar walking Cadbury.

He waved to us. "Hello, ladies. Are you out for an evening walk?"

Emily bent down to pat Cadbury, who rewarded her by slobbering over her hand.

"Actually," I said, "we took your advice. We've been investigating the manor, trying to uncover more about Kateryna's death."

"Good," he said. "Hopefully you'll discover what really happened to the poor girl."

"Would you like to come back to my place for tea and a chat?" I asked. "We have information we'd like to run past you."

"Thank you. A cup of tea would be most welcome on a chilly afternoon. Plus, I've learnt something else. Although I'm not sure if it'll help or confuse things more."

"Milk, Oscar?"

"No, thank you. Do I smell Earl Grey? My favourite." He pulled out a chair at my kitchen table and sat. "It's a nice place you have here. Right on the seafront. I've often walked past this house and wondered what it looked like inside."

"I found it on an accommodation website and rented it for a fortnight until I find something more permanent."

I placed the mugs of steaming Earl Grey on the table, swiped a pad and a pen from the top of the microwave and joined Emily and Oscar. Cadbury curled up next to the heater, sighed loudly and closed his eyes.

"Right. Regroup. Oscar, we need your ex-police experience. We were hoping to chat with Josh and see if he had any information which would help identify the murderer. What's the longest the police can hold him without charge?"

"The answer to your question is 24 hours, but..."

"Great!" I jumped up. "They arrested him on Sunday morning, so they had to release him by now. Where does he live? We could go now."

Oscar waved his palm at me in a 'sit down' motion. "Save your excitement. The police have successfully applied to hold Josh another 48 hours."

I flopped back in my seat.

"That's quite common when they're investigating a serious crime, such as murder." Oscar sipped his tea. "But here's the strange thing." He lowered his voice. "Despite the fact I saw them together several times myself, Josh told the police he was never Kateryna's boyfriend."

Emily and I looked at each other.

She raised her eyebrows. "Why would Josh say he wasn't Kateryna's boyfriend? She was pregnant by him."

"Was she?" asked Oscar. "Hmm. Is he trying to deflect suspicion? I'd observed them walking together in the High Street. And I saw her by his father's fishing boat, chatting with him."

"Grantley Bramhall confirmed he'd seen them together too. He said he'd chased Josh out of his house with a shotgun."

"Did he just?" asked Oscar. "I wonder if the police are aware of that?"

"Let's work on the theory that they had a relationship," I said.

Oscar nodded. "So, what did you discover at Redcliff Manor?"

"More questions than answers. We talked to Grantley and his personal assistant, but I can't say we obtained anything useful from either of them, apart from confirmation that Grantley was convinced Josh had killed Kateryna, and he told the police to arrest him."

"Grantley's a regular donor to the police charity," said Oscar. "And he sponsors the Police Winter Ball."

"Are you saying the police are taking bribes from him?" I asked.

"Not cash-in-the-back-pocket bribes. Perfectly legal ones, if you understand my meaning. Did you discover anything else?"

"I enacted a cunning plan." I flicked my hair back and grinned. "We secretly scoped out Kateryna's bedroom."

Oscar smiled and furrowed his brow. "Are you sure you're not an undercover detective? Not that I, um, approve of sneaking around private premises without permission." He leant forwards on his clasped hands. "Do spill the beans. This is most exciting. What did you find?"

"A mystery. Kateryna owned some very expensive possessions. She had a Vivienne Westwood dress..."

"Oh my goodness," said Emily, clutching her chest, "you should've seen it. Shimmering silvery-white, with sequins. It was like something you see movie stars wear on the TV."

"...and Jimmy Choo shoes," I continued, "and a necklace featuring several large diamonds."

Oscar pursed his lips. "Where on earth would they have come from?"

"We wondered if she'd stolen them. But, although I met her only once, I didn't think she was a thief. She didn't have that aura."

"Hmm." Oscar picked up his tea again, frowned and set it down. "Did you find anything else? An Armani handbag, perhaps?"

"We didn't find a handbag. Only the clothes you'd expect a stable girl to wear, letters from her family, books in Ukrainian, and a *Red Carpet Superstars* magazine.

"And some chicken," giggled Emily.

"Oh yes." I grinned back at her. "And some chicken."

Oscar leant back in his chair. "All right. You've assembled several clues. Now we have to work out how they lead us to a murderer. Who's our prime suspect? Who has the most obvious motive?"

I puffed and shook my head. "I wish I was an undercover detective. I still can't think of a reason why anyone would want to kill a young, Ukrainian stable hand."

"Let's start with the biggest clue," said Oscar. "Who, potentially, could've been the father? Who might've had a motive to prevent the birth?"

"Josh would have been my prime suspect," I said.

"Humour me," said Oscar. "Let's keep an open mind and say it wasn't him. Who else?"

"Nigel, the chauffeur?" said Emily. "He's probably around 45, and not the most attractive man. Like a little weasel. I can't imagine Kateryna wanting to have a relationship with him."

"Maybe she didn't want to?" Oscar tapped the pad. "Write it down. Anyone else?"

"Grantley Bramhall," I said. "Actually, thinking about it, he's a prime suspect. Estranged from his wife, a middle-aged man with pots of money, Kateryna could've easily fallen for his charms."

"Now we're getting somewhere," said Oscar. "Any other males living there?"

"There's Charlie," said Emily. "The Ferrari lunatic. But he lives in London and brings young ladies down to his father's country estate to impress them. He probably had nothing to do with it."

"I'm inclined to agree," said Oscar. "We might be able to discover if he was in town on the night of her death." He tilted his head to one side. "By the way, how did you inveigle your way into Redcliff Manor?"

"We pretended to be requesting donations for Redcliff Marine Rescue. We borrowed a collecting tin shaped like a boat from Murph. I'll show it to you. D'you have it, Emily?"

"No. Do you?"

We stared at each other, and simultaneously had the feeling that something had gone terribly wrong.

CHAPTER TWELVE

"Where's the collecting box?" I said. "I gave it to you."

"I don't have it." Emily glanced around the kitchen. "We must've left it at the manor."

"You're kidding. And what's this 'we' business? You left it, not me."

"I wouldn't have lost it, if you hadn't had this crazy idea to visit the manor in the first place."

"Stop," said Oscar. "Fighting amongst ourselves isn't going to help solve this murder. Retrace your steps mentally. Because if you left it in Kateryna's bedroom, which is probably some kind of crime scene, we're going to have some explaining to do."

"Okay," said Emily. "We arrived at the gates. Shiraz had the collecting box. She handed it to me when she pressed the buzzer and the big dogs arrived."

"Big dogs?" asked Oscar. "How did you deal with them? No, wait. Tell me later."

Emily continued. "I must've passed it to you, Shiraz, when we reached the front door because you were holding it when Nigel dropped his one coin in."

"Right. But then I gave it back to you while we were admiring the painting."

"Oh, yes. I was keeping it in front of me as some kind of protection from Grantley Bramhall appraising my assets."

"Then we walked through the house, out of the back door and into the stables. Did you have it then?"

Emily spread her thumb and forefinger across her forehead. "No. I don't think I did."

"Me neither. Which means we must've left it in the kitchen."

"Oh, no. Now someone'll find it there, they'll know we were snooping around, and they'll call the police, and we'll be arrested. This is a disaster." Emily clasped her head in her hands.

Oscar smiled. "Quite the opposite. This gives you an excuse to return. You could pretend you meant to leave it, so you could collect it full of money later. There are two members of the household you haven't seen yet: the housekeeper and Charlie."

"Return? Back to Redcliff Manor?" Emily shrugged. "But we weren't supposed to be where we put it."

"We can say we were looking for the bathroom," I said. "That's why we left the collecting box in the kitchen."

"When can we return? We'll only be able to stay long enough to grab the collecting tin and leave."

"I, um, have a suggestion," said Oscar. "On Friday evening, it's the Police Charity Ball. I'm invited, as is my wife. Grantley Bramhall, as a major benefactor, is bound to be there, and because there's a dinner with wine, his chauffeur will drive and wait for him. Sometimes, Nigel's lucky enough to be invited in. Old Mrs Kilpatrick will be left at Redcliff Manor alone, and you could ask her some questions. She might know whether Charlie and Kateryna had any contact, for instance."

"Oscar, you're a gem. That sounds like a plan. Emily, are you busy on Friday evening?"

"Shh." I put my finger to my lips. "There's a car coming. Hide."

We stood in the dark lane leading to Redcliff Manor, tucked into the farmer's gate. I wore my ankle-length, black coat, definitely too smart for nocturnal adventures in muddy lanes, but excellent for concealment on a moonless night. Emily had found a dark-blue jacket, navy jeans and black Wellington boots.

Headlights approached through the hedgerows, and we turned our backs to the road. The Rolls Royce cruised past, and I watched its red brake lights illuminate, then the orange flash of an indicator glowed, and the car turned out of the lane.

Silence.

An owl called in a nearby tree.

"Ready?" I asked.

We marched to the manor entrance, where we found the wrought-iron gates wide open.

Emily grabbed my arm and pulled me back. "What about the dogs?"

"The gates are open, so the dogs must be locked away. Maybe they're in the rear yard? We'll walk up to the front door, ring the bell and ask for the money box."

"You make it sound so easy."

"It will be. Trust me."

The gravel drive crunched as we approached the manor, and somehow in the dark the noise seemed louder than when we'd visited previously.

Two glass coach lights illuminated the front steps, one mounted either side above the lions.

The rampant lions.

There didn't seem to be a doorbell, so I banged the heavy, brass knocker three times.

We waited.

And waited.

"There's no one home," said Emily. She turned and began to head back down the steps.

I grabbed her coat's hood. "Not so fast, Miss. Perhaps the housekeeper's hard of hearing?"

I banged the knocker again.

We waited, then heard a metal chain rattling inside. The door opened a few inches and stopped, as a security latch arrested it.

"May I help you?"

All I saw was the wrinkled end of a nose.

"Good evening, madam. We're volunteers from Redcliff Marine Rescue. We visited earlier this week and dropped off a collection tin. We wondered if we could pick it up. Hopefully full of donations?"

"D'you have identification?"

I made a show of patting my coat, ready to explain that we didn't, when I felt something small and hard in the outside pocket.

The keyring Murph gave me at training. Yes!

I shoved it at her. "Here. This is my marine rescue, um, tag."

She took it, and the door closed. I heard the chain slide, then the door reopened wide enough to show her slight, stooped frame.

119

"Come in. I haven't seen collectors from Redcliff Marine Rescue in decades. My husband was a skipper there, over forty years ago, rest his soul. Things were different then. Ladies weren't encouraged to join. I'm Joan Kilpatrick, the housekeeper here for the last sixty years."

She inspected Emily and me, and I wasn't clear whether she approved of female emergency service volunteers or not. "Do you women actually go on the boat," she asked, "or do they just let you fundraise?"

I laughed briefly. "We're fully fledged operational volunteers, and we'll be out on the water this weekend."

"Will you indeed? How long have you been doing that?"

"We joined recently. I'm new in Redcliff-upon-Sea, staying at Melville Cottage, on the seafront. Emily runs the Wicked Whelk café."

"Well, well, well." She shook her head, and I wondered if we'd found a secret ally. "I thoroughly approve. We need more young, fit volunteers like you two. The sea's a dangerous place. Only last week, a poor girl drowned in West Cove."

Bingo.

I pursed my lips and nodded. "We heard something about that, didn't we Emily?"

"Terrible," said Emily. "Did you know the girl?"

"Of course. Her name was Kateryna. She worked here. And"—she checked around as if the hallway contained hidden microphones—"she had a secret. A secret that consumed her every waking moment."

Double bingo.

"She did? Goodness. What kind of secret?"

The old housekeeper extended her neck towards me and half-whispered, half-mouthed, "She was pregnant."

Drat. I knew that.

"Oh, really? Did she tell you?"

"It takes a mature woman to spot these things. She couldn't conceal it from my experienced eyes. And she confided in me. I know who the father is."

Triple bingo with knobs on. Be nonchalant, Shiraz.

"Oh, do you? How interesting."

"What job did Kateryna do here?" asked Emily.

Gaaah. Zero bingos. Bang goes our chance. I glared at her.

"She looked after Mr Bramhall's three horses. I do wish he'd find someone else to help. I can't be mucking out horses at my age."

"No, of course not. Was she employed full time?"

"Yes. She added up the books as well. But she was hopeless at that. Nigel Whitmore, Mr Bramhall's assistant, told me he had to correct all her mistakes. Anyway, I'd better not hold you up. What was it you came to collect?"

"A money tin. Shaped like a boat."

"Oh, yes. I found it in the kitchen and put it somewhere in the study. Let's take a look there."

She creaked a side door open, and I heard the click of a light switch. The three of us entered a large, high-ceilinged room with curtained, tall windows in two of the walls.

Every inch of wall space was covered in paintings. Paintings of people. Some were clearly very old; some were merely painted in an old-fashioned style. The red, patterned carpet was barely visible under a huge collection of furniture: Chesterfield sofas, dark-wooden occasional tables with spindly legs, intricately detailed urns as tall as my waist. Scattered in between the antiquities were buff-coloured folders of papers, piled ten high. A path led through the clutter to a heavy, solid, antique oak desk in front of one of the windows, and another path permitted access around the perimeter of the room, where the full-length, heavy drapes had been drawn, their golden, decorative ropes dangling at their sides.

"Goodness," said Emily. "I've no idea how anyone finds anything in here."

"Mr Bramhall knows where everything is, I'm sure," said the housekeeper.

I need to investigate this room. But how am I going to distract her? I know.

"Emily, you're interested in art."

"I am?"

I clenched my teeth and glared at her. "Yes. Didn't you study at art college? Isn't your hobby old paintings?" I winked and really hoped she'd get the message.

She winked back.

Phew.

She pointed at one of the pictures. "Who's this chap? He looks very important, seated on that horse."

"You have excellent powers of deduction," said Mrs Kilpatrick. She led Emily around the edge of the room, behind the Chesterfields. "He was indeed important. That is the Earl of Rotheringshire, who stayed at Redcliff Manor back in the 1700s. The portrait was commissioned to mark the occasion. Mind you, I've heard people say he was plumper than he's depicted, and the artist flattered him considerably. Whereas the painting next to him is..."

Her explanations and Emily's mutterings of agreement faded into the background, as I made my way over to the desk. As soon as I leant over it, I spotted our collection tin and quickly secreted it under a pile of newspapers.

Two large, leather-bound books lay open on the desktop. I glanced at columns of figures. Despite over twenty years since I'd studied accounting at school, I knew what I was looking at; standard double-entry book-keeping. Very old-fashioned now in these days of computers, but still a perfectly valid way to track revenue and cost.

Emily made a brave effort to look fascinated while Mrs Kilpatrick held up a small silhouette portrait to the light.

I leant over the pair of books.

One was dated last year. The other the year before.

Two piles of invoices lay adjacent. The top sheet of each was identical, except in the right-hand one, someone had whited out the date.

The second sheet had received the same treatment.

And the third sheet.

I rubbed my face. This didn't make sense.

I sat at the desk, seated in what must be Grantley Bramhall's chair and ran my finger down the columns of figures in the left-hand book. Quick-and-dirty mental arithmetic informed me they all added up correctly.

The other book also added up correctly.

The curious thing was, they both added up to the same number.

These aren't real accounts. No business has identical expenses each year.

I stood, grabbed the money tin and waved it above my head. Nigel's one coin clattered around the inside.

"Found it," I called. "Thank you so much."

Emily and Mrs Kilpatrick turned around to look at me.

"We must be going," I said, taking Emily's arm and steering her away from a large painting of a man holding a gun and two dead pheasants, with a pair of spaniels at his feet. "It's very late."

"Are you sure?" said Mrs Kilpatrick. "Emily, you must return one day, and I'll show you more of the collection. Most of them were on the walls when I arrived here sixty years ago. Mr Bramhall likes to pretend they're his ancestors."

"Oh, I'd love to," said Emily, in a voice that clearly indicated she wouldn't.

"Thanks, Mrs Kilpatrick." I waved to her as we skipped down the front steps.

"Yes, and thank you for showing me all the paintings," said Emily. "They were, um, fascinating."

"Goodbye, my dears. Good luck with marine rescue."

She closed the door, and we stood in the light of the two coach lamps.

"Now what?" said Emily. "If I see another picture of a man on a donkey, I'll scream."

"You're the donkey, Emily. Mrs Kilpatrick was about to tell us who the father of Kateryna's baby was before you cut her off. She said it was a secret that consumed her every waking moment."

125

Emily crossed her arms over her chest. "Sorry. I thought I was asking a sensible detective question."

Our feet crunched on the gravel away from the house towards the gates into the lane.

"Now we'll have to find a way to interview her again. Drat, drat, drat. I can't tell if she's on our side or not. She said Kateryna made mistakes with the accounts, and Nigel had to correct them. From what I saw in the study, the accounts were immaculate. Nobody corrected them. Someone's mis-using the data, and I think I know who it is."

"Is it Nigel?"

"Either him, or...quick! Duck down."

I grabbed Emily and pulled her into the bushes, as car headlights swept across the drive.

CHAPTER THIRTEEN

Car tyres crackled on the gravel, and I dragged Emily behind a significant rhododendron.

"Who's that?" she asked. "It can't be Grantley and Nigel. The Police Ball won't be finished for hours."

We peeked through the leaves as a low-slung, red, sports car swept into the drive and skidded to a halt.

I gasped. "Charlie Bramhall."

"Great," said Emily. "We can interview him as well."

"We can hardly spring out of his father's shrubbery and ask him where he was on the night in question, can we? Do be sensible, Emily."

"Ssh. He's turning off the engine. Oh. And he has company."

A blonde girl of around eighteen wearing a minuscule, black dress and little else jumped from the passenger seat. As she leapt out, we heard a mobile phone ring.

"Go inside, Taylor," said a male voice from the car. "Wait for me in the bedroom." A bunch of keys jettisoned from the driver's window, and the blonde plucked them off the gravel and ran up the front steps.

"She looked so young," whispered Emily.

"Ssh. He's answering the phone."

We heard the conversation through the car's speakers.

"Hello?"

"Charlie? Hi, Babe. It's Alex."

"Ppf," breathed Emily. "Another of his many girlfriends."

I prodded her. "Shh. Listen."

"Oh. Hello, Alex. Um, what are you up to?"

"I'm with my parents at the Police Ball. Your dad's here too. It's as boring as listening to paint dry. Please save me. Rescue a damsel in distress? You could collect me, and we could hang out." We heard a sing-song in her voice. "I'm wearing your favourite underwear."

"Um, I'd love to. But I'm, err, not in Redcliff. I'm in London."

"You told me you'd be in Redcliff this evening. I've been desperate to see you all week."

"Sorry, Alex. Change of plans. I might be down next weekend. Call me then, okay?"

"But…"

A click indicated the conversation had ended. Charlie Bramhall jumped out of the Ferrari, clunked the driver's door closed and jogged up the steps.

"Sounds like Taylor's getting lucky tonight and Alex isn't," said Emily, as we stood and brushed dead rhododendron leaves from our clothes.

"Alex must be Alexandra Flaxworth-Mills, the daughter of the local politician. Grantley wants Charlie to marry her."

"Doesn't sound like Charlie's interested. He lied to her and said he wasn't in Redcliff."

I felt something solid under my shoe and bent down to run my fingers over the gravel. A metallic object responded to my touch, and I picked it up. "Emily, shine your phone torch. What's this?"

She removed her iPhone from her pocket, and I threw my hand over my face as a pinpoint of white light pierced my eyes.

"Not at me, silly, at this." I waved the metal item.

"It's a horseshoe."

"Why would a horseshoe be next to Charlie Bramhall's car, on Redcliff Manor's drive?"

"Maybe someone was riding earlier, and it fell off?"

"It looks brand new."

"Bring it with us," said Emily. "It might be a clue."

The pebbles crunched beneath my bare toes as I sprinted across Redcliff's beach towards the sea in my swimsuit. My favourite one with the pink tassels. I jumped in and dived, rising to the surface and spluttering. My father waded in with me, grabbed me and threw me over his shoulder. I ducked under again.

I turned, grinned and waved to my mother on the beach. Our Corgi, Poppy, refused to get wet and stood on the shore, barking at me. I called her. I wanted nothing more than for her to swim with me. But she wouldn't come and stood barking.

And barking.

And barking.

Sweat dripped off me as I woke with a start. The curtains flapped gently in a draught that oozed through cracks in the window frames. I threw back the covers and peeked out of the window, watching a man on the pebble beach throw a stick to his dog, who chased it and woofed excitedly.

Why did I dream of my childhood? My parents? Poppy?

My eyes closed as I desperately tried to hold on to the dream.

The breeze blew the bushes flat as I strode west towards the location where my childhood holidays had played out. Staying in a wooden cabin, me, my parents and my dog. Those cabins were long gone, smashed by a huge landslip years before. I couldn't tell exactly where they'd been.

But I knew where the beach in my dream was, although every year, the winter storms changed it. Some years it was almost entirely sand. Some years, pebbles with patches of sand.

Today, it was pebbles with patches of pebbles.

Stumbling over the grey stones hurt my ankles, and I continually changed direction, dancing between areas of smaller, smoother shingle. The waves crashed to my left as my route took me into the spray zone.

The cold mist made me feel alive. I stretched my arms above my head, laughed loudly and spun around in a circle.

Energised.

Free.

Free to be me.

I wasn't Shiraz the accessory for a photo.

I wasn't Shiraz, the failed model, the clothes horse.

I wasn't Shiraz, the wife who provided a public face to the man who, all the time, had been carrying on an affair with his personal assistant.

I was Shiraz, the little girl again. The gangly, too-tall-for-her-size-eight-swimsuit girl who loved to play in the waves, run in the sea, build sandcastles on the beach with her dog.

Innocent, happy, childhood activities.

A middle-aged couple stared at me in disbelief as I ran up to the water's edge and desperately tried to dip my fingers in the salt water without getting my shoes wet.

And failed.

And didn't care.

I stood on the shore with my hands on my hips, gazed to the distant horizon and pretended I could see it through an eight-year-old's eyes.

But I couldn't.

The weight of the last three decades had eased since my return to Redcliff, but I could never shake off the history of all that had happened.

Never become that eight-year-old girl again.

I turned to the right and continued my walk.

The beach ended at the promontory, and my thoughts returned to the past, running around to West Cove at low tide with my father, dodging the biggest waves, successfully reaching the other side, then running back quickly before the tide turned and cut us off.

Today the water was too high to consider it. I resolved to study the tide tables and identify a time when I could investigate there.

My neck extended as I stood back and gazed up at the perpendicular, red cliffs. The cliffs which gave the town its name. At the top, tufts of scrub protruded and waved in the breeze.

Maybe there'll be a clue up there, where I last stood with Kateryna?

The bushes blew across the beginning of the cliff path, almost concealing it from view. I pushed them aside and began the ascent. My feet weren't as familiar with the track as Kateryna's had been, and I tripped on tree roots. I frowned to myself as I remembered my chase after her, wearing my wedges. Today's sneakers were far more practical. The trees crowded in, and I twanged the branches out of my way. Brambles snagged at my trousers, and I paused to unpick them. As I burst out into the meadows at the summit, I frightened a rabbit which sprinted down a hole under a tree, flashing its white tail.

The wind blew stronger at the top of the cliff. I bent my head into the gale and marched forward, following the edge, the ocean to my left; the meadows to my right. Sea mist descended, and I peered in the direction of Redcliff Manor, but the distant buildings were obscured. I crossed the promontory and reached Kateryna's favourite spot, directly above West Cove.

I'm her. I'm Kateryna. And I'm speaking with each potential murderer in turn.

I closed my eyes and imagined Josh standing in front of me. I'd no idea what he looked like, but I knew he was a young fisherman, so I guessed his appearance and came up with a bearded male model I'd seen in a magazine about sailing, wearing a Breton shirt. I was pretty sure Josh didn't wear a Breton shirt, but this image would suffice for the exercise.

"Josh, I've something to tell you."

"What?"

"We're going to have a baby. You'll be a father."

"Don't talk rubbish. We always used protection. You're not having a baby."

"I am giving birth, whether you like it or not. Even if you don't like it, I'm keeping him. Or her. If it's a boy, I'm naming him after my brother who died in the war."

"You're not keeping it. I've saved some money. I can help you pay."

"No! Never. I thought you'd be so happy we were going to be a family. I hate you."

I opened my eyes.

This was a theory I'd never considered. This single-actress role-playing was working rather well. I pulled out my phone and typed: *Josh bashed her and threw her from the cliff, due to disagreement about the pregnancy.*

Pregnancy.

The word took me back twenty years. I shook my head rapidly. Time to focus.

Who's next? Grantley Bramhall.

I closed my eyes and pretended to be Kateryna again.

"Grantley, we can't keep meeting. This affair's never going to work. I'm 23. You're over 50. You're a rich landowner; I'm a stable hand. I've enjoyed our little dalliance, but it's time to end it."

"No, Kateryna. I don't care. I'll give up my house, my Rolls Royce, my life here to be with you. I love you."

I opened my eyes. *Stop, Shiraz. Run that one again. We went a bit Mills and Boon.*

I put myself in Kateryna's shoes once more, shut my eyes and imagined Grantley Bramhall standing in front of me.

"Grantley, we have to end this affair. I'm 23; you're 50. It's been fun meeting secretly, but this isn't what I want."

"It's what I want, Kateryna. You're a fine-looking filly. My wife's away in the city, and a man has his needs."

"No, Grantley. Let go of me. I have to tell you something."

"What?"

"I'm pregnant, and I don't know whose it is."

"Are you saying it could be mine?"

"It could be."

"That's ridiculous. I can't be fathering another child. Your baby would lay claim to Charlie's rightful inheritance."

"Grantley, what are you doing?"

"Nothing. I just thought you might like to take a closer look at the sea. Isn't it, how shall I put it, striking?"

I opened my eyes again. This was really good. Grantley had killed Kateryna because they'd had an affair, and he didn't want his precious son Charlie's inheritance to be challenged.

I typed this theory into my phone.

Two seagulls soared on thermals. I stared at them as they floated on air and thought how Kateryna would never again be able to sit up here and watch them. Watch her friends the birds.

Time for suspect number three. Nigel.

I closed my eyes for the fourth time and channelled Kateryna.

"Why did you ask me to come here, Nigel? You said you wanted to talk to me in secret."

"Keep your nose out of things that don't concern you. There's nothing wrong with the manor's accounts. The only reason I have to redo them is because you make so many mistakes."

"That's not true, and you know it. The reason you redo them is that my book keeping's perfect and shows up your little scheme. Does Grantley know about this, or does he trust you with the money? Are you siphoning off his wealth into a private account of your own? I'll find out; you know I will."

"You won't find out if you fall off this cliff. Everyone knows you come up here to sit by yourself. What if you had a little accident?"

"No, Nigel. Get off me. Leave me alone."

I opened my eyes again. Of all my play-acting theories, this seemed the least likely. Nigel was a slight little man, built like a jockey. Kateryna would've been a match for him. She could've defended herself.

Last suspect. Charlie.

I closed my eyes, but I couldn't imagine the scene. My eyes squeezed tight as I tried to force it to come.

Nothing.

I couldn't think of any scenario where Charlie Bramhall would kill Kateryna.

I wasn't sure they even knew each other.

In the harbour below, the Redcliff Marine Rescue boat left the shed and launched. I knew Murph would be taking three of the new recruits out for their first experience of on-water operations. I hoped they'd all taken seasickness tablets; it looked choppy today, although a watery sun peeped through the grey clouds.

The tide had fallen since I'd come up here, and half of West Cove was now above the waterline.

I gazed down at the pebble beach, and a glint of light on metal shone back at me.

Then the sun hid behind the clouds, and I didn't see the reflection again.

My stomach rumbled, and I decided to head to Emily's café for brunch.

Every table at the Wicked Whelk was occupied that Saturday brunchtime, but not with fishermen. Young families and couples escaped the winter weather and clutched steaming hot coffees and chocolates.

Emily dashed from the kitchen to the tables, balancing breakfasts of cooked egg, bacon, mushroom and chips, toast with little jars of honey and jam, porridge sprinkled with cinnamon and muesli, chopped fruit and Greek yoghurt.

She called over her shoulder as I closed the door behind me. "Hi, Shiraz. Bit busy today. Usual double shot skinny latte?"

"Yes, please. In a takeaway cup."

She imitated a recorded announcement. "You are caller number three in the queue. Please hold."

I laughed as she fired up the coffee machine and grabbed two slips of paper from a clip above it.

"Have you had a good morning?" she asked, as steam hissed from a nozzle.

"An interesting one. D'you want to come around later, and I'll tell you about it?

"I could visit this evening? I have to go to the wholesaler in Headland Bay this afternoon."

"Okay."

She waltzed past me with two hot drinks and placed them in front of her customers.

"Is there a fish and chip shop in town?" I asked her. "I could grab some, and we'll have them tonight."

"Yep. 'The Plaice To Be', on Middle Lane, leading off the High Street. It opens at five, I think."

"Great. Shall I pick up a bottle of wine too?"

"Better not. We're out on the boat tomorrow. If the weather's anything like today, we won't want a hint of a hangover. I'm buying a crate of lemonade from the wholesaler; I'll bring a couple of cans. Here's your coffee. I'll see you tonight."

"Okay. Bye." I picked up the drink, turned around and found myself face to face with Nigel. Not quite face to face; he's about two feet shorter than me. But you know what I mean.

"Hello, Marine Rescue charity collector," he said. "Will you be paying us a further unscheduled visit, or are two sufficient?"

CHAPTER FOURTEEN

Nigel smirked, and I disliked him more.

D'you have any idea I've uncovered your little creative accounting scheme? And you're on my list of murder suspects?

"I don't know, Nigel. Am I able to persuade you to donate another single coin?"

"Unlikely. Money's tight. Times are hard."

Maybe that's why you're cooking the books. Are you embezzling Grantley's fortune?

Nigel slitted his eyes. "Mrs Kilpatrick told me you seemed very interested in our stable hand who passed away? Tragic events, but you're going above and beyond saving lives at sea, aren't you?"

"Does her death mean something more to you than merely having to collect the pastries on your day off?"

"Why do you care? You didn't know her." He pushed past me and approached Emily behind the counter.

I shuddered, opened the café door and headed for home.

The Plaice To Be sold me two huge fish and a large portion of chips. As the man wrapped them in sheets of greaseproof paper, I wondered whether one would've been enough.

The smell of the food reminded me of evenings with my parents, sitting on the beach, watching the sunset, eating fish and chips with our fingers.

My mother always complaining, as my father liked vinegar on his chips, and she didn't.

I loved vinegar, so she was outvoted. I loved tartare sauce too, but my parents always forgot to buy that.

Tonight, I'd made sure I had some in stock.

Emily knocked on my door shortly after six. I'd laid the table with two place settings, set the oven to a low temperature and slid the food inside to keep it warm.

"This is very homely," she said, placing four cans of lemonade on the table. "Sorry, these aren't cold. They come in a slab of 24 from the wholesaler, and I forgot to stick them in the fridge."

"We're in luck," I said. "This accommodation has a freezer." Emily pinged the cans open, poured their contents into the two glasses, and I plopped ice cubes into each one.

We sat down, clinked our tumblers together and laughed.

"Cheers," said Emily. "Here's to a great day tomorrow."

"Yep. I can't wait to go out on the bright-red boat, crashing through the waves, the salt splashing on my face. D'you have much boating experience, Emily?"

"You'd think I would have, being a fisherman's daughter. But I was never allowed out on the boat with Dad. He said it was too dangerous an environment for me. Despite growing up by the sea, my experience is limited to inflatable dinghies. How about you?"

"I learnt to sail as a teenager. Thornhill Grange Ladies College offered it as a sport, and we used to go to a lake and spin around in little wooden yachts."

"Your school gave sailing lessons? Goodness. Mine didn't even teach swimming."

"Um, I attended a private school. We did rock climbing, orienteering, even skiing."

"You're so lucky," said Emily. "Did you play a team sport? I was good at netball."

"Me too. I was the shooter, because of my height. And I played hockey."

My knife parted the flakes of fish. They were as white and chunky as I remembered them from my childhood and, as soon as I popped some in my mouth, they melted. The golden batter crunched satisfyingly, and I squeezed the fresh slice of lemon the shop had provided.

"How long's that fish and chip shop been there?" I asked. "This fish tastes as good as it did thirty years ago."

"As long as I remember," said Emily. "Although it's changed hands several times. The new people renamed it. Last year it was called 'The Codfather'."

I covered my mouth to avoid spitting chips over the table. "I love these corny shop names. My friend had a dog training service called 'Sit Happens'."

Emily chuckled. "What d'you reckon about Murph and his funny sayings? They always make me giggle. He pretends he's getting so annoyed, but I think he's having a laugh. 'Galloping galleons' and 'Bloodthirsty bowsprits'; he reminds me of a cartoon pirate."

I laughed again. "What d'you think he'll come up with tomorrow? We must remember to return the money box, now we've retrieved it."

"With our one coin. We'll need to think up a story as to why we didn't collect more."

"Or we could put some money in ourselves? I have change from the fish and chips."

The collecting tin rattled as I banged it on the table. As I peeked in the slot, I noticed something in it that wasn't a coin.

"Emily, there's a note in here. Paper money."

"Really? Maybe it was already in there when Murph gave us the box."

I shook the tin upside down. "How does this open? How do we get the money out?"

I twisted the boat-shaped container around in the light. The red top was the same colour as the real rescue boat, and the underside was white.

Emily took it from me. "Maybe there's a join in the middle." She felt around the edge with her fingernails.

"If there is, it's invisible. It's very well made."

She gripped the top and the bottom, grimaced and pulled.

Nothing.

"Shall I have a go?" I asked.

She passed it to me, and I repeated her action, with identical results.

"I think you're right," I said. "I saw a tiny crack when we tugged it. Let me find a sharp knife."

Rummaging in a drawer produced a huge cleaver which a butcher might've used to dismember a cow, and I briefly wondered why temporary accommodation always seemed to contain these random, useless items.

"Okay," I said. "You hold the box on its side on the table, and I'll force this knife in here and twist it into the crack."

"Um, don't cut my arm off."

"Hold it at the ends. Then I won't hurt you. Ready?"

Emily grasped both ends of the collecting tin. I wiggled the chopper into the crack where the red colour and the white colour met and pushed.

145

"It's coming," she said, clenching her teeth. "The crack's getting bigger."

I heard the snap of a plastic clip.

"Keep going," said Emily.

The boat suddenly gave way under the knife's pressure, and I fell onto the table and knocked over both glasses of lemonade.

"Drat. Grab a tea towel from the sink. It's a good job they weren't full."

"Lucky I brought spares." Emily wiped the lemonade up. She laughed and held up a copper-coloured disc of metal which had rolled under a plate. "Here's Nigel's coin. D'you have a mop? The floor'll be sticky."

"I've no idea. I'll clean it with a cloth for now."

As I bent under my chair to wipe up the mess, I found a small, white scrap of paper on the floor, damp from lemonade.

"Emily, look. This must be the piece of paper from the collecting tin. It's not money, it's a note." I passed it to her and pushed myself up.

She held it by one corner. "It's a very soggy note."

"What does it say?"

She spread it out and dabbed it with the tea towel.

"The evil's factory is in Jerusalem." She showed it to me. "Is this some kind of coded message? Have we uncovered a religious plot? All the time we believed this murder to be about Kateryna's pregnancy, but it's really about something much more sinister?"

"Calm down. You're being sensational. Let's work this out before jumping to conclusions."

"Sorry," said Emily. "I'm considering all angles." She peered at the paper again. "D'you have a magnifying glass?"

"I doubt it."

"You didn't know you had a meat cleaver until you looked." She began opening drawers in the kitchen and extracted yards of brown string, notepads and a pair of scissors. "One magnifying glass," she said triumphantly, brandishing the object at me.

"Wow. I'd never have guessed."

I switched on my phone's torch, and we inspected the paper on the table.

"There's another letter before 'evil'," I said, pressing my finger on the paper. "What word ends in 'evil'?"

"Weevil?" suggested Emily. "The weevil's factory is in Jerusalem?"

"That doesn't seem very likely."

We sat and picked at our leftover chips.

"This has me stumped," I said. "Maybe it really is 'evil'. Maybe the letter before it's smudged ink."

We jumped at the sound of three knocks on the door.

"I'll clear away while you get that." Emily picked up the plates.

The front door opened to reveal Oscar and Cadbury, who shook himself and tugged his master into the hall in a desperate effort to greet me.

"Hello, Oscar, what brings you here?"

"As I took Cadbury for his evening walk, I saw the lights on, and I thought I'd knock. I have some news. A mystery, really."

"Come in. Emily's here too. We also have a mystery. Let's try to solve them together."

"Something smells good," said Oscar. Cadbury rushed into the kitchen and hoovered up a dropped chip.

"We've just finished our takeaway. I would've bought more if I'd known you were coming."

"Thank you. My dinner'll be waiting for me when I get home. So, what's your mystery?" He pulled out a chair and sat down.

"We went back to Redcliff Manor, saw Mrs Kilpatrick and retrieved the collecting tin. You were absolutely right; she was there by herself."

"Well done. Did you discover anything else?"

"Emily managed to persuade her to show her some paintings in Grantley Bramhall's study. While she was explaining who they all were…"

"Boring old men on horses," said Emily.

"…I took a peek at the desk in there. It looks like Mr Bramhall's running two sets of accounts. There's something dodgy going on. One set seems correct; the other's a duplicate but with the invoices re-used. Kateryna said she did the books, but the second set's in different handwriting."

"Is that your mystery?" asked Oscar.

"No. There's another one. Mrs Kilpatrick told me she knew the name of the person who got Kateryna pregnant."

"Really?" said Oscar. "That ties in with what I have to tell you. Who is it?"

"I don't know. She was about to tell me when Emily interrupted."

"Sorry," said Emily. "I thought I was helping."

"Never mind. You made up for it by looking at all those paintings."

Oscar cleared his throat. "So you saw Mrs Kilpatrick, had a sneaky look at the study, and left with the money box?"

"Yes. But, when we forced it open, this flew out." I slid the piece of paper in front of him.

"Sorry, Shiraz. I don't have a hope of reading this without my glasses. What does it say?"

"It doesn't make any sense. We think it says, 'the evil's factory is in Jerusalem'. But there might be another letter before 'evil'. Emily suggested 'weevil' but 'the weevil's factory is in Jerusalem' makes even less sense. Can you think of any other words that might end in 'evil'?"

Oscar raised one finger. "I'm a bit of a crossword buff. Let me ponder." He leant forward on his elbows and massaged his temples.

"Devil? That's all I can come up with."

"Of course. Devil. The devil's factory is in Jerusalem? That doesn't help us either."

"Maybe the note's a red herring?" said Emily. "Maybe it's left over from something years ago."

"I wish I had my spectacles," said Oscar. "You don't have a magnifying glass, do you?"

"Um, funny you should ask." I handed it to him, and he moved the magnifying glass closer and further away from the paper.

"I'm sure it's 'devil'," he said. "The devil's factory is in Jerusalem. Although I've no idea what that means." He held the paper up to the light and peered through the glass. "There's something else here. A watermark in the corner. It has a picture and some writing around it, but I can't make out what it is."

He passed me the paper and magnifying glass, and I looked. "The paper's torn through where the watermark goes, but there's a building in the middle then, encircling the building, above are the letters R-E-D and below are the letters M-A-N. Red Man?"

Oscar pursed his lips. "Grantley Bramhall must own watermarked notepaper. I reckon 'Red Man' is one half of Redcliff Manor."

"Redcliff Manor notepaper. So we know this note came from Redcliff Manor, and wasn't in the money box before we visited. But what does it mean, who put it in there and why?"

"That remains a mystery," said Oscar. "Shall I tell you my news now?"

"Ooh, yes, please. What have you come up with while we were snooping around the manor last night?"

"The news is, the police have successfully applied to hold Josh a final 48 hours without charge."

"Oh," said Emily. "I was so sure he was innocent."

Oscar shrugged. "He may still be. There's another piece of news too. He's adamant he wasn't the baby's father, and he's allowed the police to perform a DNA test. They don't have the results yet, though."

"Gosh. That is news. How do you find out all this stuff?"

Oscar tapped the side of his nose. "Anyway, all it tells us, is that Josh probably didn't get her pregnant. It doesn't confirm he didn't kill her."

"I still say he didn't," said Emily.

"I've never met him," I said, "so I can't say one way or the other."

At that moment, the sound of breaking glass came from the living room.

"Cadbury," shouted Oscar to the air, "what have you knocked over?"

"It's not Cadbury," said Emily. "He's lying in front of the oven."

I stood, opened the kitchen door and peered into the hallway. The living room door was open and, for some reason, I could feel a draught coming from it. I switched on the light and screamed.

CHAPTER FIFTEEN

"Oscar, Emily. Help! Come, quick."

I ran to the broken window and looked out, then wondered if this was a good idea. Cold air funnelled through the smashed pane, and the sea sounded louder than it should do indoors.

"What happened?" asked Emily, as she rushed in with Oscar, who failed to prevent Cadbury from joining us. "How did the window break?"

Oscar picked up an object from the carpet. "It's a horseshoe. Careful, both of you. Out, Cadbury. Shards of glass are everywhere. D'you have a vacuum cleaner?"

"I'll look in the cupboard under the stairs." I threw my hands in the air. "Why would someone throw a horseshoe through my window? Goodness knows how I'll explain this to the landlord."

Emily wagged one finger. "Someone's sending us a message. Warning us off."

"Indeed." Oscar nodded. "If the murderer threw this, it means we've rattled them. We're on the right track."

"Goodness. Should we tell the police?" I asked.

"Maybe not," said Oscar. "You have your suspicions about people at the manor. Remember, Grantley Bramhall's friendly with the sergeant. We don't want him to find out anything about our investigation."

"Perhaps," said Emily, "we could feed the police some misinformation. Call them around to report the broken window, then tell them we know who did it. That might make the killer expose themselves."

I squeezed her shoulder. "Emily, you've been reading too many Agatha Christie books. This might not be connected with the murder. Local teenagers might've found this horseshoe in the street and thrown it through the window for a prank."

"Who do we know who has access to horseshoes?" asked Oscar.

"Everybody. There are three horses at the manor. All our suspects do. Except Josh."

"Josh could've thrown the horseshoe to deflect attention from himself?" said Emily.

"Um, Emily. There's a problem with your theory. Josh is still in police custody."

"Oh, yes. So it couldn't have been him."

"He's only locked up until tomorrow morning," said Oscar. "The magistrate won't grant them a further extension unless they charge him, and their case is becoming flimsier and flimsier."

He looked at his watch. "I must go home before dinner's burnt. D'you need any help to clear up?"

"We'll manage," I said. "Thanks for coming around."

He grabbed Cadbury's lead, and they left.

"Could I stay the night here?" asked Emily. "I'm scared. Whoever threw the horseshoe might come looking for me too."

I hugged her. "Of course. There's a spare bed in my room. We can go to training together tomorrow."

"Thank you. I don't suppose you have a spare toothbrush?"

"As it happens, I have spare everything. The landlord left a welcome pack, but I brought all my own toiletries so I haven't used any of it. Let's clear up this mess, shove something over the hole in the glass and get some sleep. We've a big day tomorrow. First time on the boat."

Sunday morning found me bouncing out of bed, throwing open the curtains, standing in front of the window, feet apart, hands on my hips, breathing deeply and smiling.

Today was the day.

Today, for the first time, I'd do what I'd set out to, when I escaped the city and returned to my childhood holiday town to build a new life.

A life where I did things that mattered.

A life where I wasn't just arm candy in *Red Carpet Superstars* magazine photos.

A life where I made a difference.

Where I helped people.

Rescued people.

Saved their lives at sea.

And in the process, saved my own life.

Today was the day when Murph would take us new recruits out on the boat.

Emily opened her eyes, stretched and glanced left and right. "Hi, Shiraz. I forgot where I was for a minute."

"You're safe here with me, and no-one's tried to attack us in the night."

"I'm glad I'm with you. You're a good friend."

"So are you. Right now, us good guys need to stick together. We'll have to put our investigation aside today, while we learn marine rescue skills."

"D'you reckon we'll rescue anyone today?"

I stared out of the window. The light-blue winter sky ended at a band of cloud on the horizon. A procession of three fishing boats departed from the harbour and chugged across a lightly choppy sea. Waves rippled onto the pebble beach. "I doubt it. The water'll be freezing. Nobody apart from the fishing people will be out today. Murph said most jobs happen in the summer, when the tourists get blown out to sea on inflatable flamingos, swans and pelicans."

Emily and I laughed at the vision of an armada of giant, plastic birds bobbing across Redcliff Bay.

"He also said when the pager goes off in winter, it's serious. Someone's life's in imminent danger. A walker's cut off by the tide, or someone's fallen in the water."

"Like Kateryna."

"Yes, like Kateryna." I bit my bottom lip at the thought of a young life cut short, and silently resolved to avenge her death by finding her killer.

We tugged on clothes, arranged our hair so it didn't look like we'd just got out of bed, threw down some disgusting, instant coffee and headed for the marine rescue station.

I made sure to double-lock the door as we departed.

"Morning, ladies," called Murph. His voice echoed from inside the rescue boat mounted on its trailer. "Grab some protective gear. Your personal kit won't be ordered until you complete probation, so help yourself to any of the outfits which don't have a name on them." He pointed at an open door to the side of the shed marked 'Locker Room'.

I followed Emily and took one step backwards as I noticed a man sitting on the central bench in between two rows of metal cupboards.

Ooh. The tall, curly haired chap who helps Murph with his computer.

"Morning," he said. "Emily, isn't it? I'm David. You run the café, right?"

"That's me. From memory, you have a takeaway flat white with one sugar."

I laughed. "D'you know everyone by their coffee order?"

"Only if they're consistent." She introduced us. "David, this is my friend, Shiraz."

"Are you coming out with us today?" I asked.

"I am. The boat requires a minimum of a skipper, that's Murph, and one qualified crew, which is me. Until you're qualified, you'll need to be accompanied."

"How many can she carry?" asked Emily, glancing up at the red vessel.

"Eight, maximum. We had five yesterday, with the other three trainees. It'll be less crowded with four today. We won't be bumping into each other."

Emily and I pulled on waterproof trousers and jackets. "Boots," she said.

I searched around the floor. "Yep, I'm finding a pair my size."

"No, Boots. He's behind you."

I turned as the cat smooched around David, and he tickled his ears.

"I forgot to feed him last night as I stayed at Shiraz's," said Emily. "Have we got five minutes for me to pop home and find him something?"

"All good," said David. "I brought some meat for a barbecue after training. He's consumed a chunk of steak."

Boots purred like an outboard engine, as Murph shouted from the shed. "Tangling turnbuckles. Is anyone coming with me today, or am I launching this vessel alone?"

As soon as we left the harbour, the red vessel bounced across the sea away from the land. Some waves were bigger than others, and every few crests Murph called out for us to hold on. This was my first time on a real, sea-going small boat. Millionaires' yachts didn't count; you didn't feel connected with the ocean on them. More like connected with privileged idiots.

"Wow," I said to Murph, as he gripped the wheel, and I grasped a handrail. "The front of the boat dipped right under."

"Suffocating sail-lockers. Not 'the front'. Didn't you listen to anything at training on Monday? The vessel's forepart is called the bow. And the back is called the stern."

Emily poked me and said quietly, "Left is port and right is starboard."

"Thanks. I remembered that bit."

I gazed towards shore at the higgledy-piggledy lines of houses climbing the hill behind Redcliff's seafront. Everything looked different when viewed from the water; it became obvious that the High Street wasn't straight; it possessed a slight elbow in the middle which wasn't clear when you walked down it. I identified Melville Cottage in the centre of the seafront, a slim, pink building sandwiched between other cottages, all painted in different colours.

The red cliffs bookended both sides of the town; tall, wide placards of terracotta topped by green meadows with cliff paths. A line of ant-like walkers ascended towards a summit.

Murph spoke over his shoulder. "The first thing you'll learn as new crew on the vessel is watchkeeping. The skipper can't look everywhere at once, so it's your job to alert me to anything I may've missed."

"Fishing boat on the starboard side," I shouted.

"And one on port," called Emily.

"Very good." Murph nodded. "I was aware of those, because we're cruising through the fishing grounds, but if in any doubt, call it out."

I waved at a yellow-jacketed fisherman on the deck of a trawler as we passed, and grinned as he waved back at me.

He greeted me because I'm a fellow ocean worker. Not because I'm a bikini-clad jewel posing on my husband's yacht.

Murph pulled back the throttles and idled the vessel's engines. "Time for a drill. I'll preface it with the words 'this is an exercise', so no-one's in any doubt. Out here on the ocean, it's very different from the classroom. Everybody ready?"

I gulped and tried to remember anything about Monday's training.

David winked at me. "It doesn't matter if you make a mistake. That's why we train."

"This is an exercise," boomed Murph's voice, so loud in the confined cabin that, even though I'd expected him to say it, I flinched, and Emily grabbed my arm.

"We've had a report from the Coastguard of a missing paddle boarder. We know they set off from the harbour, and they were planning to paddle across the bay to the east end of Redcliff's main beach. The journey should've taken thirty minutes, but they've been gone over an hour and their partner's reported them missing. There's a light offshore breeze."

He paused. "First, where would they be most likely to end up?"

"If there's a light offshore breeze," said Emily, "they'll be blown out to sea. Towards where we are now."

161

"Correct," said Murph. "What would be the best way to look for them?"

"Binoculars?" I asked. "Do we carry them?"

"We do," said David. He tugged a pair out of a holder and passed them to me. I felt a tingle of electricity as our skin touched.

I lifted the binoculars to my eyes, stared through the lenses and swung them around. Magnified versions of waves, hills and a fishing boat passed through the viewfinder.

"These are very hard to use at sea," I said. "Even if I focus on something, the boat's bobbing up and down too much."

"So what are the chances of you seeing a person in the ocean?" asked Murph.

"None at all."

"Correct. Binoculars aren't very helpful when searching for something in the water. Any other ideas?"

"We could each stand in a corner of the boat and sweep our gaze over different parts of the sea?" suggested Emily. "That way, we'd cover more search area than if we were all looking in the same direction."

"You're getting closer," said Murph. "Think about your last sentence. Covering more search area."

We stood silently and pretended to think. I flicked my eyes at David, who I could see was bursting to tell us the answer.

"David," said Murph. "D'you want to put these new recruits out of their misery?"

"We'd commence a parallel search," said David.

I leant in to hear his explanation.

"Imagine the sea's a huge lawn, and our boat's a lawnmower. We know the paddle boarder's between here and East Beach, and he or she's hopefully no further away from shore than where we are now. So we'd drive in a straight line, parallel to the shore, with all four of us looking in both directions, just like you described, Emily. Once we reached the west side of the bay, we'd head in towards shore one hundred yards, then head back the other way. We're mowing the sea, and we'll cover every bit of water with our eyes. With each pass, we'll come closer and closer to shore and hopefully, at some point, we'll find the paddle boarder and pull him or her onto the boat.

"Let's practise it," said Murph. "I'll watch forward to port, David'll watch forward to starboard, and you both can watch port and starboard aft." He winked. "That's the back of the boat, Shiraz." He pushed the throttles, and the vessel headed steadily in a straight line. The rescue boat rose and fell with each oncoming wave. I gripped a handrail, and my pulse quickened as I gazed at the all-round ocean.

This is what I dreamt of doing. I'm making a difference, training to save lives at sea.

David called, "Turning starboard ninety degrees in 5,4,3,2,1." The vessel turned and headed directly for shore, then David's voice sounded again. "Starboard ninety degrees in 5,4,3,2,1." Our path parallel to the shore was restored but heading exactly in the opposite direction. Just as if we mowed the sea.

We completed a further four passes, coming nearer to shore each time. The cold, winter air kissed my cheeks, and I felt energised and alive. I imagined searching for real, scanning the sea for a missing person, finding them before the waters condemned them to an early grave. Bringing them home safely to their loved ones. My mind drifted to Kateryna, and how she'd never return to her loved ones. Her poor parents, who'd now lost two children. And with their remaining son fighting in a war, how must they feel?

"Stop," called Emily. "I see something. On the port side."

"Really?" asked Murph. He set the throttles to neutral and brought the vessel to a gentle halt. "Where?"

She pointed with her left arm.

Murph rolled his eyes and shook his head. "Emily, that's the starboard side."

"But it's on my left. You said left was port."

"Port is left when looking ahead. When you're facing aft, it's on the right."

"This is confusing." Emily rubbed her hair. "And I don't see anything now. Maybe it was a breaking wave?"

"After a short time on a search, maybe only twenty minutes, your eyes start to see things," said David. "You think something's in the water, but it isn't. If this was a real search, we'd have more crew on board. More eyes to relieve each other. Especially at night."

Murph stepped away from the wheel. "So we learnt that the monotony of searching plays tricks on our eyes. The water all looks the same after a very short time. What else did we learn from this exercise?"

I blushed. "Um, I started to lose concentration. My mind stopped focusing on the search, and I began to think about something else."

"Don't be embarrassed," said David. He laid one hand on my shoulder. "It's hard to keep your mind on the job when searching. This is why we practise, so when we have to do it for real, we can mentally prepare. No one can search continually."

He smiled at me, and I smiled back.

I jumped, as the radio crackled into life.

"Marine Rescue Redcliff, this is Coastguard Headland Bay, come in please. Over."

CHAPTER SIXTEEN

"Marine Rescue Redcliff, this is Coastguard Headland Bay, come in please. Over."

"That's the Coastguard base for our area," explained David. "They must have a shout for us." He plucked the radio handset from its clip and spoke.

"Coastguard Headland Bay. This is Marine Rescue Redcliff. Go ahead. Over."

"We have a report of a person in the water at West Cove. Are you able to assist? Over."

"We are able to assist," said David into the transmitter. "ETA twenty minutes. Over."

"Proceed immediately to West Cove," said the radio. "I repeat. Proceed immediately to West Cove. Contact us on channel sixteen when at the scene for further instructions. Over."

"Marine Rescue Redcliff proceeding immediately to West Cove. We will contact you on Channel sixteen on arrival. Over."

"Coastguard Headland Bay out."

"Hold on, everyone," said Murph. "This'll be bumpy." He pushed the throttles forward, and the tone of the engines rose.

Emily and I gripped overhead rails as the vessel scooted across the waves at top speed. With each jarring crash, something incorrectly stowed, such as a pen or a plastic cup, flew from the boat's dashboard and struck the floor. I glanced down at where these objects fell, then quickly looked up again as impending nausea forced me to watch the horizon.

"This is a Mayday, right?" I yelled at David, who sat in the navigator's seat beside Murph and grasped a handle. He kept a careful watch forward.

"Yep. Someone in the water on a freezing winter's day is definitely a Mayday."

"The second one this month," shouted Murph. "What's going on?"

"Will we arrive in time?" I stared at the screen in front of him which displayed a chart in various shades of blue, a symbol of a boat, which I presumed was us, and a black line extending directly forward from the symbol towards the top edge of the screen.

"Who knows?" Murph yelled above the crashing and splashing. "It depends if they're fully immersed and trying to stay afloat, if they have a lifejacket, if they're wearing a wet suit or a dry suit. We don't know yet if this is an old man who's fallen off the cliff or a young, fit, kite surfer who's in trouble. The outcome could be very different."

"It might be a false alarm," shouted David. "Sometimes people on top of the cliffs see a seal, or even rubbish, like old clothing, and they call it into the Coastguard as a person in the water."

"The job we had last week; we thought it would be something like that," said Murph. "But it wasn't."

I squeezed my eyes closed at his reference to Kateryna, then opened them as nausea returned.

Emily spoke. "Did you retrieve last week's body from the ocean yourselves?"

"Nope," said Murph. "Volunteers aren't allowed to recover bodies. We leave that to the Coastguard. The paid professionals."

I heard a whump-whump-whump, frowned and gazed back at the engines. "What's that noise? Is something wrong?"

"It's the Coastguard helicopter," said David. He craned his neck forward and pointed through the windscreen. "They'll reach West Cove before we do."

"So why we were told to go?" asked Emily.

David turned his head towards her and yelled. "In an emergency, they want all available assets as close as possible to the action. We don't have enough information yet to know what might happen. There may be an upturned boat, or multiple casualties. Or the helicopter may need our help."

"Assets?"

"Boats, helicopters, rescue equipment. Even us volunteers. We're an asset."

I smiled briefly to myself.

I'm an emergency service asset.

The cliffs appeared through the sea mist. I tried to orientate myself as to exactly where we were, but the bouncing vessel prevented any activity apart from holding on tight. Murph slowed the engines, and the boat bobbed and swayed a short distance offshore.

To our right, the town of Redcliff showed as an outline. From this angle, it looked different; the harbour wall had a strange curve that didn't look right. Most of the town was hidden behind it.

To our left, the red cliffs curved around the coast.

Directly in front of us we saw West Cove. I stepped out onto the rear deck and heard the thumpety-thumpety of the helicopter as it hovered above the beach. A shaft of sunlight shone on the cliffs and the meadows above. I realised that, 24 hours previously, I'd been standing on top of them, looking back this way.

Murph's voice called from the wheel. "David, grab the radio and tell the Coastguard we're on scene."

David unclipped the handset. "Coastguard Headland Bay. This is Marine Rescue Redcliff. Over."

"This is Coastguard Headland Bay. Go ahead. Over."

"We're on station two hundred yards off West Cove. Awaiting further instructions. Over."

"Marine Rescue Redcliff, please dispatch a crew member to the beach. I repeat, please dispatch a crew member to the beach. The helicopter will lower a paramedic who will need your help. Over."

"Received. We will dispatch a crew member to the beach to assist a helicopter paramedic. Over."

"Thank you. Coastguard Headland Bay out."

"Sounds like you're going for a swim, David," said Murph. "We'll veer down and get you as close as possible."

My eyes opened wide, and I stared at David. "You're going in the water? In these waves?"

"Yep. This is what we train for." He checked the zips of his dry suit.

Murph drove the rescue vessel slowly towards the breakers, as the helicopter hovered. The boat circled, so it pointed away from the beach, then the clankety-clank of the anchor chain banged from the bow.

"Ready, David?" asked Murph. "The beach shelves steeply here, so I'll drop you around thirty yards offshore."

"Ready."

"Be careful," I said, then immediately wished I hadn't.

David cupped a hand to his ear. "Pardon?" he yelled. "I can't hear you over the noise of the helicopter."

I blushed and shook my head. "Nothing."

David called to Murph, "Permission to open the boarding door, Skipper?"

"Permission granted."

"Opening boarding door." David swung a section of the boat's side open, grasped his white helmet, jumped overboard and disappeared under the waves.

Two seconds later, I was relieved to see him bob to the surface and swim backstroke towards the shore, while Murph closed the boarding door. Emily grabbed my arm and pointed at the helicopter. We looked on, as a figure wearing orange overalls dropped on the end of a string. This didn't seem real, as if we were watching a 1970s stop-motion scene from *Thunderbirds*. Something else dangled with them.

"What's the helicopter person holding?" I asked Murph.

He grabbed binoculars and raised them to his eyes. "A collapsible stretcher. To recover the casualty. Or the body, if we're too late."

Emily pointed again. "Look. Onlookers on the clifftop."

"Could I have the binoculars?" I asked.

"Of course." Murph gripped my arm to steady me. "Hold the binoculars in one hand and the vessel with the other. One hand for yourself and one for the ship. We don't want you tumbling overboard; you're not trained to do what David's doing."

David stumbled out of the waves onto the beach, and I smiled slowly as he marched through piles of seaweed. My eyes found the helicopter in the binoculars' vision as the boat swayed, and I followed the winch line down.

"The paramedic's on the shingle with David," I said. "And the helicopter's retracted the line, and it's circling."

"Let me look," said Emily. She grabbed the binoculars and stared at the action on West Cove. "Ooh. They're lifting something onto the stretcher. It's a person."

"Can you see who it is?"

"Not from this distance. They look like a trussed-up Christmas turkey."

"Lifting doesn't sound good," said Murph. "That means even if the casualty's alive, they're not able to help themselves."

"There's hardly any land left," said Emily. "They were both knocked over by a wave."

"The tide's coming in," said Murph. "And it's a spring tide. They need to get out of there with the casualty before they run out of beach."

"What's a spring tide?" I asked.

"Very high and very low. They happen every two weeks, at a full moon or a new moon. This evening's tide will be low. A lot of beach will be exposed. The opposite's a neap tide, where it's not so high and not so low."

"The paramedic's strapping the person to the stretcher and attaching a harness," shouted Emily. She puffed out her cheeks.

I stared directly upward as the helicopter passed so close I felt I could reach up and touch it. It took up station in its previous position above West Cove.

"Now the helicopter's dropping the line onto the beach again," continued Emily's commentary. "The paramedic's attached it. They've extended their right arm horizontally. What does that mean?"

"Ready to winch," explained Murph. "They must give clear arm signals to communicate with the winch operator."

"Can't they call each other on mobile phones?"

Murph laughed. "You'd never hear a phone call above the helicopter's rotors. Plus, there's no mobile signal in West Cove. It's a comms shadow."

I frowned. "If there's no mobile signal, how do people in trouble call for help?"

"A mobile phone will often connect with the emergency number if there's no signal. You could even take the SIM card out of your phone and still make an emergency call. They work on a different channel."

The paramedic and stretcher elevated from the beach together and dangled at the end of the rope, which gradually became shorter as the winch operator wound them upward.

We watched as they reached the helicopter, a crew member helped them through, the door slid closed and the helicopter flew to the east.

Usual noise levels were restored, and we no longer had to shout at each other. I leant over the stern of the rescue vessel and watched David trudge down the beach and swim towards us through the waves. Several times I held my breath as the crests broke over him, and his white helmet disappeared in the troughs.

Murph unlatched the boarding door and attached a metal ladder to the opening as David approached. He pulled himself up with his strong forearms and knelt on the vessel's deck.

I crouched beside him. "Are you okay?"

"I'm exhausted." He glanced up at me and panted. "The cold water slapping your face really saps your energy."

Murph produced a steaming mug and handed it to him. "How's the casualty, David?"

"Not good. Unconscious; barely breathing. Looks like they took a tumble."

"Gosh." Emily puffed. "I didn't expect that on our first boat training, hey Shiraz?"

"Nope. I was so impressed with how the emergency services work as one. I can't wait until we've completed training, and we operate as seamlessly."

"You'll never complete training," said David, pushing himself to his feet. "We're still learning every day."

Emily passed the binoculars back to Murph, and I intercepted them. "Could I have a quick look through these?"

I pointed them at the clifftop. The crowd of onlookers had dispersed, but two figures remained, hands in pockets, staring back at our vessel.

And I recognised one of them.

CHAPTER SEVENTEEN

"Marine Rescue Redcliff, this is Coastguard Headland Bay. Over."

David back into the cabin as the radio sparked into life.

"Coastguard Headland Bay, this is Marine Rescue Redcliff. Go ahead. Over."

"Stand down. I repeat, stand down. Over."

"Received. Marine Rescue Redcliff standing down. Over."

"Thank you for your assistance today. Coastguard Headland Bay out."

"I have to say," said Murph, "that's the first time I've received a serious shout with brand-new crew on the boat. You were lucky to experience that."

"Luckier than the poor person on the beach," I said.

"D'you reckon they fell off the cliff, like the girl last week?" asked Emily.

"Probably." David nodded. "Or they could've been cut off by the tide and then hurt themselves trying to navigate the promontory. You can only reach West Cove on foot at a low spring tide. They probably walked there first thing this morning, then tried to make their way back when it was too late. People swim around on calm days in summer, but it'd be lunacy to try that today."

"We'll head back to base and debrief," said Murph. "I need a cup of tea after that."

"And a steak sandwich," said David. "Who's hungry? I've marinated the steaks in garlic and herbs; they'll taste great straight from the barbecue."

Emily tangled herself into knots pulling at her wet weather dungarees, and all my muscles were employed trying to strip off my waterproofs.

"Emily, could you give me a hand? I can't reach the Velcro at the back of my neck."

I felt David's firm grip on my shoulder as he tugged the strap free and pulled it down to my waist.

"Thank you." My cheeks reddened. "I don't normally have trouble undressing myself."

"I hope they managed to take that person to hospital in time," said Emily. "How terrifying, with the cliffs behind them, the raging sea in front of them and the beach disappearing bit by bit. I can't imagine how it'd feel. I'd be in major panic."

"Now you know the danger," said David, "you'll never put yourself in that situation. If you do venture into West Cove, you'll make sure the tide's falling."

"I used to swim around there as a child," I said. "On calm, summer's days. With my dad."

"You did?" David tilted his head. "I thought you'd recently moved here."

"It's a long story. We used to holiday in Redcliff-upon-Sea when I was a child. Then I spent most of the rest of my life in London. And now I'm back."

"For good?"

"Hopefully. I need to find somewhere to live. I only have my temporary accommodation until the end of next week."

Murph stumped in holding a steaming cup, set it down and stripped his outerwear off with a fluid, effortless motion. "Did you learn anything today, ladies?"

"I learnt port and starboard are different when you're looking forwards and backwards," said Emily.

"Meddlesome marlinspikes. Ahead and aft. Not forwards and backwards. Next time we're on the boat, we'll run through that part of training again."

We laughed.

"What did you learn, Shiraz?"

"I learnt it's hard to concentrate when on a search. And I learnt you can make an emergency call from any mobile phone, even if it doesn't have signal."

"Very good."

"I learnt something too," said David.

"What did you learn?" asked Murph.

"I learnt I have two nice new crewmates." He grinned at me and Emily, and I blushed.

"Emily, are you busy this afternoon?"

We sat at her apartment's little dining table and nursed cups of tea. I picked at a muffin she'd produced, and melting chocolate chips stuck to my fingers.

"I have some meal prep to do for the café tomorrow, but that'll only take an hour. Why, what d'you have in mind?"

"When you were looking through the binoculars at the helicopter, did you see that crowd standing on the clifftop?"

"I noticed people up there, but I was too busy trying to work out who was on the stretcher. Why?"

"After the helicopter had gone, the onlookers dispersed, but two people remained staring down at us. I'm sure one was Grantley Bramhall, but I couldn't see who the other one was; they wore a tight hood around their head."

"Maybe it was Nigel?"

"This person looked stockier, more heavily built." I took a deep breath. "I want to investigate West Cove."

"Woah. Are you completely insane?" She held up both palms towards me. "We've just watched someone winched half-dead from there by helicopter, and you're going to put us in their position? No way. If you're planning to visit West Cove, you're on your own." She paused, and bit her lip. "Although, I'd prefer if you didn't go at all. I don't want you to die."

"Calm down, Emily. Nobody's going to die. We understand how the tides work. It's spring tides, right? Very high and very low. So long as we nip around the promontory as the tide's flowing out and keep our visit brief, we'll be fine. We'll check the tide times on the Internet."

"Why d'you want to go there, anyway? Haven't we had enough excitement for one day?"

"Yesterday morning, before I bought my coffee from you, I went for a walk by myself on the cliffs above West Cove."

"Nice. Blow away the cobwebs."

"I wanted to penetrate the killer's mind, and I wondered if standing where the murder happened would help."

"Did it?"

"I'm not sure. I pretended to be each suspect, having a conversation with Kateryna. I played both parts, and walked through the conversations as they might have happened."

"Goodness. Were you an actress as well as a model?"

"I knew several actresses, but it was never my forte."

"Did you come to any conclusions?"

"Not really. I pretended I was Josh, then Grantley Bramhall, then Nigel. I ran through what might've happened with each one. I even pretended to be Charlie, although I'm sure it wasn't him who killed her. He wasn't in town to my knowledge."

"So why d'you want to visit West Cove? D'you think she was actually killed there?" Emily covered her mouth briefly. "Ooh. She wasn't pushed from the cliff? Someone took her around the promontory at low tide and left her to drown?"

"Nope. Remember when Murph came into your café and told us the Coastguard had recovered a body? He said it was high tide. So they were definitely pushed. The reason I'm going to West Cove is that I saw something from the cliffs. Something shiny on the beach, which didn't look like it belonged. It might be a clue."

"And it might be a piece of rubbish. Why put your life at risk for a tin can?

"Emily, are you with me or not?" I stood and thumped the table, which made Boots jump a foot in the air and hide behind a cushion. "Are we going to carry on with the investigation, clear Josh's name properly and discover who the police should really be talking to, or are we giving up now? Because I'm not giving up. Not now, and not ever. I know what it's like to be young, pregnant and scared. I know what it's like not knowing who to turn to. I know what it's like feeling very, very alone."

My teeth clenched, and I turned my face sideways briefly, then back again. "And I know that Kateryna did not deserve to die for the crime of becoming pregnant to the wrong man. So, Emily, are you coming? If not, I'm walking around that promontory by myself, and I'll find out who killed her."

My eyes watered, and I took a deep breath, while Emily stared at me with her mouth agape.

She stood and pushed her chair in. "Shiraz Jones, you're one fired-up, determined woman, aren't you? Let's do this."

She hugged me, then we bumped fists as if we were in a gangster movie.

The wind and waves had abated as we strolled away from the harbour to the promontory. We'd spent the afternoon chopping sandwich fillings together in the café and discussing our respective suspicions as to the identity of the murderer. At least, Emily had chopped sandwich fillings. I contributed by passing her slices of bread.

I still reckoned the answer lay at Redcliff Manor. But who was the mysterious figure standing with Grantley Bramhall? And what was the shiny object I'd seen on the beach? The answer to the second of those questions would be found at West Cove.

The sea rippled gently at the foot of the promontory, and a slim section of beach was exposed, consisting of small pebbles and larger, seaweed-covered rocks.

"It's 4:30 p.m. What time's low tide?"

"The website says 4:47. We have half an hour to nip around, find whatever you saw and come back again."

"Ready?"

Emily sucked in a breath. "Ready."

We clambered over the slippery rocks. At one point, I slid, my foot splashed in a rock pool up to my ankle and I discovered how freezing the sea was on this winter's afternoon. After several minutes of being mountain goats, the secret world of West Cove opened up to us.

Emily gasped. "I haven't visited this beach since I was a little girl."

"Me neither. Look! The cave. D'you remember the cave?"

"Yes! With the secret ledge where you could climb up and pretend to be a smuggler."

"That's it." I pointed. "And the two big rocks which the sea rushed between. I used to dodge and jump the waves there."

"Me too."

"C'mon," said Emily. "Let's explore the cave to see if it's changed."

We rushed to the back of the cove, where the cliffs met the pebble beach. Emily stuck her head around the cave entrance and called, "Hello-oo."

"OO-Oo-oo," came back at her.

"It still echoes the same as it did thirty years ago," I said. "I'd forgotten about that. WOOOO."

"WO-Oo-oo," repeated the echo.

We entered the cave and scrambled over the rock formations. "D'you reckon we played together when we were kids?" I asked. "We're not that different in age, and I came down on holiday every summer."

"We might've done," said Emily. "But even though we lived here, I only came to West Cove once or twice. My parents wouldn't let me explore here by myself. They told me horror stories of children eaten by giant, black sea monsters to frighten me away. I've no idea why they didn't just explain about the tides?"

"Maybe they figured sea monsters would scare a child off more effectively."

"Look; here's something." Emily held up a dainty chain, enveloped in seaweed.

I took the object and scraped the weed from it. "This isn't what I'm looking for. It's not big enough. It looks like a lost necklace." I slipped it in my pocket.

Emily returned to the cave entrance. "Let's find your big, shiny object and head back. I've no desire to be eaten by the giant, black sea monsters."

"How long do we have?"

"Twenty-five minutes, now."

"We'll split up. You take this part of the beach, and I'll take the far end. Look for anything man-made. Anything that shouldn't be here. Let's do a parallel search, like we learnt in training today. We'll meet in the middle."

Emily began hunting among the rocks, while I headed for the opposite side and worked my way between the rippling water and the cliffs.

I'd no idea what we were looking for, only that I'd seen a glint of sunlight reflect from something on the beach.

Something metallic.

"Found it," shouted Emily. She held up an object which I couldn't identify, so I ran across the pebbles to see what it was.

She gripped a rusty pram wheel as if she were steering a car.

I took the wheel from her and twisted it in my hand to try to find a shiny bit. "I don't think that's what we're looking for. This has been in the sea for ages. It's too tarnished to reflect light. Let's keep looking."

I turned around and discovered I couldn't easily identify which parts of beach I'd covered in my parallel search, so I started again. I walked back and forward, eyes on the ground ahead. A large, dark-green crab waved his pincers at me, then darted under a boulder. Patches of light-coloured sand showed between the seaweed-covered rocks. I realised, even if whatever I'd seen was here, there'd been three high tides since I'd caught a glimpse of it from the clifftop, and it could easily be hiding under one of these piles of black seaweed.

I looked at my watch. "Emily, we need to go before the tide cuts us off. We'll return at the next opportunity and search again."

She gazed at the sky. "It'll be dark soon, anyway. We can't search in the dark."

We strode to the end of the beach where the route around the promontory led back to Redcliff.

The water was already several feet deep.

CHAPTER EIGHTEEN

"Help. How did that happen?" I cried. "I thought we had thirty minutes."

"So did I. Could we swim it?"

"You're joking. The water's freezing. And we'll be bashed to death against the rocks."

"We can't stay here while the tide's coming in. We'll drown. I'm going to swim."

"No, Emily. Stop. We've at least an hour until the beach is covered. Maybe more. We'll call for help."

She looked at her phone. "I don't have a signal. Do you?"

"No." My phone also showed zero bars. "Hang on. Remember what Murph said about making an emergency call even if your phone has no signal?"

I dialled the emergency number and lifted the phone to my ear.

"Emergency. Which service?"

"Coastguard."

"What is the location of the emergency?"

"West Cove."

"Is that an address?"

"No. It's a beach, near Redcliff-upon-Sea. There's two of us, and we're cut off by the tide."

"Your name, please?"

"Shiraz Jones."

"Please wait, caller."

I heard a dial tone, then a third, male voice.

"Coastguard Headland Bay."

"Emergency operator connecting mobile 07700 900119."

"Your reference CGHB-77534. Go ahead, caller."

"Um, hi. We've been walking on West Cove, and the tide came in. We're cut off. Can you send help?"

"West Cove, Redcliff-upon-Sea?"

"Yes."

"How many people are cut off?"

"Two."

"Are either of you injured?"

"No. Cold and a little scared."

"Your names please?"

"Shiraz Jones and Emily Philpot."

"The tide has around fifty minutes until the beach is underwater. We'll reach you before then. Dress in any clothing you have with you. Huddle together for warmth. When you see help arrive, shine your phone torch so we can find you quickly."

"Okay. Please hurry."

"We'll be there as soon as we can. Call emergency again if anything changes."

"Thank you. Bye."

"Now what do we do?" asked Emily.

"We sit as far away from the water as possible and wait."

We walked towards the cliffs and sat on a boulder.

"How long will they be?" asked Emily. She scanned the skies.

"He said the beach'll disappear in fifty minutes. He also said they'd reach us before then."

"Thank goodness. I am never coming around here again, Shiraz. Sorry."

"I understand. I should never have brought you. I honestly thought we might solve this mystery."

"We can't even keep looking for the shiny object. It's too dark."

"Maybe it was nothing."

Emily clasped her hands together. "I've never been in a helicopter."

"I've flown in several. It's not as much fun as it looks, being buffeted around and thrown in all directions. I remember when one of my husband's clients took us on a ride over the River Thames in London. We twisted and turned, and I wanted to throw up, but there was no way I was going to be sick on the luxury carpet, so I puked in my handbag."

Emily laughed aloud. "You're joking."

"Nope. It was my best Louis Vuitton one too."

We both giggled, then stopped.

"I'm getting a cold backside."

"Me too." Emily stood and pointed. "Is that a helicopter?"

I jumped up. "Nope. Too high. That's an aeroplane."

We sat again.

"Is this life really better than your old one?" asked Emily. "It sounds so glamorous, living in the city, attending all those posh events, meeting film stars. I'd love to have the opportunity to do something like that. But I never will, living here."

"Honestly, it's not as great as it sounds. I could never be myself; I was always owned by someone. If it wasn't my husband, it was the press, or the public. Everyone had an expectation of how I should look, how I should behave, how I should treat people even if they'd treated me badly. I once featured in the gossip columns because I argued with a traffic warden, and some nosey person took a photo. You're lucky, Emily. If you argued with a traffic warden, no one would care."

"We don't have traffic wardens in Redcliff."

"A police officer, then, or a shopkeeper, anyone."

"I still think it'd be fun to dress up in beautiful clothes like the ladies in *Red Carpet Superstars* magazine and wear all that jewellery. The only jewellery I have is my mother's engagement ring."

We sat in silence.

"The waves sound nearer," said Emily. "No-one's coming, are they? We're going to drown. Who'll open the café tomorrow?"

"Don't be silly. Of course we're not going to drown. It's only been twenty minutes since we called them."

"Call them back. Ask how much longer they'll be."

"Emily, they're not a taxi service. I'll call them if we're still here, um, when the water reaches that rock." I pointed at a boulder halfway between our position and the sea.

"The moon's so beautiful on the water," said Emily, dreamily. "If I have to die, at least that'll be my last memory."

"Emily. We. Are. Not. Going. To. Die." I shook her. "Not tonight. No one dies on my watch."

"Kateryna did."

"Ouch. That was low. I tried to save her. Anyway, she died after we parted company, not while I was with her."

We sat in the darkness and listened to the rhythmic rippling, as the water grew nearer.

"There's a light offshore." I jumped up and jabbed my finger. "Maybe it's one of the fishing trawlers. Hey! Over here." I turned my phone torch on and waved it back and forth as if I were at a rock concert.

"He's showing green and red," said Emily. "And white on the mast. That means he's headed directly for us."

"Very good. Murph would be pleased with your knowledge retention."

We watched until we saw the spray from the boat's bow illuminating eerily in the vessel lights.

"Oh, no. It's Marine Rescue Redcliff." Emily rubbed the back of her neck. "This is embarrassing."

"What are you going to do, run and hide?" I asked. "Better to be embarrassed than drown."

I heard the unmistakable, booming voice of Murph carry across the water. "Can you see them, David? Grab the spotlight."

"Even worse." Emily covered her face with her hands. "It's Murph and David."

A bright beam played across the beach and settled on our faces.

"Is everyone okay?" David's voice shouted. "Nobody hurt?"

"Nothing hurt except our pride," I yelled.

"Stay there. We'll anchor and veer down."

The vessel turned around, stopped and reversed slowly until it was a short distance from the beach.

One of the shadowy figures in the boat hopped over the side. Their yellow survival gear reflected the red port light in a ghostly combination.

"What on earth?" asked David. "Murph, it's Shiraz and Emily." He waded onto the beach. "What are you two doing here alone after dark? You could've drowned."

"Um, it's a long story," I said. "I'll tell you on the ride home."

David lifted Emily and carried her through the shallows, while Murph steadied the vessel and leant over the side. He called out as they approached. "This crazy caper, Miss Emily, will cost you free bacon sandwiches for a week."

"I'll throw in free tea as well. I'm so relieved to see you; I thought we were done for."

"You almost were. Ten more minutes and you would've been underwater."

David returned to the beach. He threw his arm around me and lifted my legs as if he were a groom carrying a bride over the threshold of her new home, a not unpleasant experience.

He deposited me rather ungracefully on the boat.

I glanced back at the beach, lit up in the boat's spotlight.

And something shiny glinted back at me.

"David," I pointed. "I need to go back."

"What? Why?"

"I, um, left something important behind."

"Oh, sure," said Murph. "I'll set the meter to waiting time."

"I'm serious. I must grab something off the beach before it goes underwater."

"What is it?" asked David.

"Look where the spotlight's pointing."

The light swayed back and forth across the cliff face with the motion of the boat. Each time it reached the base of the cliff, something reflected.

"It's really important. Please?"

"Murph? Skipper?" asked David.

194

"Splintering sea-chests. I'll just hang around here. It's not like I have anything better to do."

"I'll grab it," said David. "Whatever it is. You stay here; I'm wearing survival gear. Keep warm in the cabin." He jumped over the side and waded to the shore.

The tide had advanced, and the beach was almost completely covered now, but I could still see the flash of metal each time the spotlight played across it.

I leant over the back, sorry, the stern, of the boat and watched his bright-yellow outfit trudge up the beach in the searchlight. His heavy boots crunched, and the little ripples splashed rhythmically.

"We're so sorry about this, Murph," said Emily. "We checked the tides before we nipped around to West Cove, and we thought we had thirty minutes, but when we tried to come back, we were too late. The tide had already come in."

"How did you check the tides?"

"On the Coastguard website. See this screenshot?" She turned her phone around and showed him.

"Sheesh. You two need some extra training. The tide tables on that website show the tides at Headland Bay. They're twenty minutes different to Redcliff. When you thought the tide was dropping, it was actually rising. You didn't have thirty minutes. You had less than ten."

"Ooh. Whoops. Sorry."

David returned and handed me the object he'd found on the beach.

"Was that what you wanted, Shiraz?"

Murph grunted as he raised the anchor and prepared to depart from West Cove. "Jostling jolly-boats. That bashed piece of scrap is what my crewman risked his life to pick up? We save lives at sea; we don't do salvage."

"I'll explain everything one day. Thank you so much, David."

The anchor clattered at the top of its chain, and Murph pushed the throttles forward gently.

The object in my hands was tarnished by the salt water and bent in the middle, but it was obvious what it looked like before its immersion.

"This could be very important," I said to Emily.

She plucked it from my hands and held it up. "I can't see properly in the dark. Could we turn the cabin lights on, Murph?"

"Absolutely not. You'll ruin my night vision, and then we'll end up on the rocks. You two haven't completed night training yet, have you? No white lights on the boat after dark."

"We'll inspect it when we return," I said.

The ride back to Redcliff Harbour looked very different from when we'd travelled the same route that morning. A clear, dark line showed where the cliffs ended, and the sky began. Occasional, solitary lights showed on shore. To our right—the starboard side, I mentally corrected myself—on the horizon, two white lights close together flashed different patterns, and I counted them. One flashed three times, then stopped. Then three again. The other flashed nine times. They both repeated these patterns.

"David," I asked, "what do those lights mean, out to sea? The white flashing ones."

"They mark a rocky outcrop called Blakey's Island. The lights on its east end flash three times quickly. That means: safe water to my east. The lights on the west end flash nine. That means: safe water to my west. The pair together mean: don't go between them. You'll run aground on the rocks."

He knows everything. I can't wait for him to share all his knowledge with me.

"And what are the flashing green and red ones ahead?"

"They mark the entrance to Redcliff Harbour. Coming in, we leave the red on our left and the green on our right. They're on the harbour walls. Murph runs night training once a month in winter. You two should put your names down for the next session. And take a stroll in daylight to find out what they look like during the daytime."

"Would you like to show me tomorrow?"

"I can't. I have a date with a cow."

"A cow? Um, what d'you mean?"

"He means he's going to work," said Murph. "David's a butcher."

The boat penetrated the gap in the harbour wall between the red and green lights, and Murph slowed the engine to a crawl. I didn't feel a bump as we touched the dock. David jumped up with two ropes and tied off both the bow and the stern of the boat effortlessly.

Murph turned to us. "Three shouts to West Cove in ten days. At least this one didn't result in a body."

"The job this morning? Did they die?"

"It's not been announced yet, but yes. A local lad. Goodness knows how he ended up where he did. He of all people would've understood tides. He's spent his entire life on boats."

Murph frowned and glanced down.

"D'you know who it was?" I asked.

"Yes, he was the son of a local fisherman. I know the father well. The boy's called Josh."

CHAPTER NINETEEN

My hand flew to my mouth. "Josh? D'you mean Josh Rawlings?"

"That's him. Did you know him? A simple soul. All he was ever going to do with his life was fish with his father. Goodness knows what his dad'll do now. He would've relied on his boy for so much. It's a hard, physical life out there on the trawlers."

"I'd never met Josh. You knew him, didn't you, Emily?"

"Only because he came in for tea and a bun with his father. A quiet lad. He sat at the table with the older trawlermen and kept himself to himself. An old head on young shoulders. I don't think he even owned a mobile phone."

"Wow. That's unheard of these days. Especially among the twenty-somethings."

"I'll see you guys at training tomorrow night," said Murph. "And I think we'll focus on tides for certain people's benefit. David, let's put this boat away and head off. I need to load my van for work in the morning."

"What d'you do for employment?" I asked.

"I run my own business. I'm a glazier."

"Ah," I said. "I might have a little job you could help me with. Can you repair small, individual panes in wooden-framed windows?"

Emily and I strolled back past the café.

"D'you want to pop up for a quick bite and a cup of tea?" she asked. "I want to see the object you've hidden under your coat that we almost died for."

"We didn't almost die. We were perfectly safe all along."

"Shiraz, I honestly think being saved by Marine Rescue from an incoming tide on a deserted beach after dark does not count as being perfectly safe."

Boots greeted us at Emily's door. He smooched around her legs and miaowed loudly.

Emily glanced to the side of her front step. "That's strange. Where's your water bowl?" She searched around the path at the front of the café, then peeked down the passageway that separated her building from the marine rescue station. "I wonder where it's gone?" She ruffled the cat's fur. "Sorry, Boots. You'll have to drink from your indoor one until we find it." She unlocked her door, and we climbed the steps to her apartment.

Emily pressed the kettle and yanked open a cake tin which contained the moistest, sultana-iest fruit loaf I'd ever seen. She cut a significant chunk for each of us and laid two plates on the table.

I slid my beach find out of my coat's inner pocket.

"What d'you think this is?" I asked.

I passed it to her, and she twisted it and peered closely. "It's a poker. A poker for a fire. A very bashed and bent one."

"A poker. What does that remind you of?"

I had a flashback to standing in Redcliff Manor's hallway in front of the giant, stone fireplace, and realised this was the missing hearth-tending tool to accompany the brush, the shovel and the tongs.

"Emily, d'you realise we might be holding the murder weapon? Remember what Oscar said? Death by trauma from a blunt object?"

She dropped the poker, and it clanked on the floorboards. "Great. Now my fingerprints are all over it. And yours. I'll spend the next 24 hours waiting for the police to knock at the door."

"How will they know whose fingerprints are on it if we've got it?"

"We're going to hand it in to them, right? We can't keep a potential murder weapon to ourselves."

"Um, okay. I'll take it to the police station in the morning. We'll say we found it in West Cove and got our fingerprints on it carrying it home. That's the truth, and if needed, Murph and David can corroborate our story."

I took my coat off, threw it over the back of a chair and sat. As I pulled the chair towards the table, something plinked out of the coat pocket onto the floor.

"What's that?" asked Emily. She placed a mug of tea in front of both of us.

I picked up the object. "It's the thing you found on the beach near the cave. It's probably rubbish. D'you have a cloth? I'll wipe it clean."

Emily passed me a damp cloth, and I rubbed the small item between my fingers. I spread it out across the table, and Emily fingered it.

"It's a locket. On a silver chain." She lifted the heart-shaped metal trinket, which wasn't much bigger than her thumbnail.

"Someone must've dropped it," I said.

"Probably. I wonder if it opens?" She grabbed a vegetable knife and slid it along a minuscule crack. The locket broke open, and drips of water fell out.

"How long's it been underwater?"

"No idea. Someone could've lost it on another beach, or off a boat; anywhere. Then the tide washed it up on West Cove where it lay hidden until we found it." She inspected the interior. "There's a photo of a young woman in there. That's quite common. In the olden days, people would carry around a picture of their deceased relatives in a locket like this." She prised the photo out with the knife and dabbed it dry.

Water damage had blotched the left-hand side of it, and a dismembered arm snaking around the girl's shoulders betrayed where someone had been chopped out of the picture.

"Do you know her?" I asked.

"I don't think so. But we've no idea how old this picture is. She could've died decades ago, perished last year or might still be alive and have grandchildren of her own."

I snapped the locket closed and slid it back in my pocket. "Maybe we'll never know." I drained my tea. "I'd best be going. This"—I waved the bent poker in the air—"should interest the police. Thanks for the tea. See you at training tomorrow night."

"Morning, Love. How can I help?"

The rosy-cheeked policeman addressed me from behind the police station's counter.

"Bert, isn't it?"

"That's right. You're Emily's friend. Her of the delectable chocolate pastries. I must find a reason to proceed in a southerly direction down to the harbour and buy one."

Sergeant Will looked up from a filing cabinet. "Bert, how often do I have to tell you? We do not 'proceed in a southerly direction' anymore. That phrase went out with flares. 'Walk south' will suffice. And please don't call our customers 'Love'."

Bert coughed and blushed.

"I came in last weekend to discuss Kateryna's death," I said to Will.

"That's right, you did. You thought it was suicide, but we knew better, didn't we, Bert?"

Bert opened his eyes wide, removed his glasses and cleaned them. "I still can't believe Peter Rawlings' son was responsible for her death. Such a well-mannered young lad. Course, I've known his family all my life. Mired in tragedy, those people. It must've been three years ago, that poor..."

"Enough reminiscing, Bert," said the Sergeant. "How can we help you today, Ms...?

"Jones, Shiraz Jones."

"That's right," said Bert. "I wanted to call you Sherry, but that didn't sound right. I knew it was something nice to drink."

Sergeant Will clenched his teeth and stared at Bert.

I decided to bring a premature end to their double act. "I have some evidence, which I believe may pertain to the case."

"What case?" Will folded his arms and frowned.

"The case of Kateryna's murder, of course."

"It's too late for evidence now," said Bert. "The murderer's dead himself. Went over the same cliff."

"Bert!" Sergeant Will thumped the table. "That information has *not* been officially released."

"It's okay, Will." I gave Bert a half-smile. "I know already. News travels quickly in a small town. But what if someone else killed her? Let me show you something."

I tugged out the bent, tarnished poker and placed it on the counter. Will picked it up and covered it with his own fingerprints. I shook my head minutely and thought he should be handling a potential murder weapon more professionally.

"What's this, then?" He twisted the poker in the light.

"It looks like an old poker," said Bert. "We had one of them when I was a child. Every morning, my mother would sweep out the hearth with a little dustpan and brush that accompanied it, then use the matching set of tongs to lift coals into a newly laid fire. Those were the days. I always say to the wife, you can't toast marshmallows over a radiator."

"Thank you, Bert, for that little portal into the past. Where did you find this, Ms Jones?"

"On West Cove, last night. In fact, rewind. I was standing at the top of the cliffs on Saturday morning, looking down at the beach, and I saw something glinting. Yesterday, I went with my friend Emily to see if we could find it. And we did. I think this might be the murder weapon, and I think it comes from Redcliff Manor."

Sergeant Will slitted his eyes. "What, exactly, are you insinuating?"

I swallowed hard. "There's a brass set of fire implements in the hall at Redcliff Manor, the same as Bert was describing from his childhood. Except the poker's missing. And"—I pointed my finger at him—"I believe you're holding it."

Sergeant Will laid the bent poker back on the counter. "Be careful what you're saying, Ms Jones. It sounds to me like you're accusing someone in the Bramhall family of murder, based on the flimsy evidence they're missing a poker, and you've discovered one that may or may not be the same poker washed up on a beach."

"That's exactly what I'm saying, yes."

Will folded his arms again. "Ms Jones. We arrested the murderer. We know it was him, but we couldn't gather all the evidence before that woolly-headed magistrate made us release him. Now he's dead, which is tragic, but it means the case is closed. We're not looking for anyone else in connection with this."

I stamped my foot. "That's ridiculous. Kateryna lived at Redcliff Manor. She was struck with a blunt object to kill her. I've discovered a very suitable blunt object close to the spot where her body was found, and this blunt object"—my voice rose as I picked up the poker and brandished it at them— "comes from Redcliff Manor. Don't you see the connection here?" My eyes filled with tears. "How d'you know Josh wasn't killed by the same person who killed Kateryna?"

"He was," said Will.

I felt a chill through my body. "What d'you mean, he was?"

"I'm sorry, Ms Jones. I thought you knew. Josh was killed by the same person that killed Kateryna. Once we'd released him from the cells, he jumped off the cliff and took his own life."

CHAPTER TWENTY

I held onto the police station counter with both hands, and my knees turned to jelly.

"Shall I fetch you a cup of tea?" asked Bert. "You've turned white, which is, um, quite a feat for a person with your complexion."

I held a breath. "Thank you, Bert. I'll be fine." I turned to Will. "What makes you believe Josh committed suicide?"

"We know he did. His father, Peter, found a note in his bedroom."

The High Street shops held no interest as I stepped slowly, one foot ponderously in front of the other, staring at the pavement, biting my lip.

Could it be true? Could Josh really have killed Kateryna then, racked with guilt, thrown himself off the same cliff?

I needed to recap, to regroup. To put Oscar's and Emily's heads together with mine.

To analyse everything we knew.

Everything.

No matter how insignificant.

No matter how trivial.

How do they do this in detective novels? Ah, yes.

I nipped into the newsagent's shop and purchased a gigantic piece of white card and a pack of coloured pens.

That Monday afternoon before marine rescue training, my usually quiet house contained four people and a dog.

Oscar sat at one side of my kitchen table with a cup of tea.

Emily sat on the other side.

I sat at the head.

Cadbury lay in front of the oven.

And whistling, and the clattering of tools came from the living room, where Murph fixed my window.

The giant, white sheet of card I'd bought from the newsagent's covered the entire rectangular dining room table, and I poised with my black, red, blue and green markers.

Oscar rubbed his hands together so hard I thought they'd steam. "This is exactly how we used to plan out investigations back in my days in the force, before computers came along and made everyone's lives harder."

"I'm glad you're on the team, Oscar." I laid one hand on his arm. "What's the best way to go about this?"

"I'd always start with the victim. Put them in the centre. Draw a circle and write their initials in it."

I leant across the table and, with a blue pen, drew a circle two inches across, wrote 'K' in it, then looked at Oscar for affirmation.

"Exactly." He nodded. "Now we need to draw circles surrounding the victim with the names of the primary suspects. Grab the notes you've made and write down absolutely everyone who could be under suspicion. But don't be ridiculous. Don't include us or the police, for instance."

"I don't know," said Emily. "That new sergeant's a bit iffy. Maybe he'd been subject to some kind of investigation in another police force and been discarded to Redcliff-upon-Sea."

Oscar raised one eyebrow in a Roger Moore gesture. "As I said, don't be ridiculous."

"Okay. First, the most likely. The people who knew her well. Grantley Bramhall, Nigel and Joan Kilpatrick."

Oscar pointed at the paper. "Draw circles for the three of them. And include Charlie Bramhall as well. We can't rule him out by any means."

I drew four circles surrounding Kateryna's and initialled them 'G', 'N', 'JK' and 'C'. "Should I include Josh?"

"Definitely. But put a cross beside him. I mean a cross like a church cross. That signifies the suspect is dead."

"Do I write a cross next to Kateryna's circle too?"

"No. In a murder investigation, it's normal to assume the victim is deceased."

Emily laughed, spluttered tea and narrowly missed the investigation sheet.

"Careful, I only bought one piece of card. What's next, Oscar?"

"Draw a line connecting each suspect to the victim. Maybe use a different colour, like black."

I pushed the top onto the blue pen, uncapped the black one and drew straight lines connecting the circles.

Emily giggled again. "Now your drawing resembles some kind of horrible one-way traffic scheme."

"Do try to stay focussed, Emily. This is a serious matter."

"Now think of any secondary suspects," said Oscar. People who weren't directly connected with the victim but may've had a reason to kill her through association."

"I can't think of anyone." I said. I absentmindedly sucked the end of the pen. "I mean, where do we stop? We can't put down Murph and David, for instance."

Oscar cleared his throat. "That wasn't what I meant by secondary suspects. Secondary suspects are people who are directly associated with the primary suspects, but don't appear to be connected to the victim."

"Such as...?"

"Peter Rawlings. Or Alexandra Flaxworth-Mills."

"Really? Where should I write their names? Do they get a circle?"

"Yep. Draw a circle for each of them near to the person they're most closely connected to, initial it, and draw a line to their corresponding primary suspect."

I drew a circle slightly outside Josh Rawlings' one and initialled it 'PR'. A second circle appeared close to Charlie Bramhall's, with 'AFM' in the centre.

"Anyone else?" asked Oscar.

I referred to my notes. "Um, Elizabeth Bramhall?"

"I'm certain she wasn't involved," said Oscar. "But put her down."

I drew the final circle. "Apart from other outliers, such as ourselves, that's everyone I can think of."

Oscar pushed his chair back, stood and surveyed our work from above. "I was a policeman for over thirty years, and I've done this exercise more than once. In my experience, somewhere on this page is the name of your murderer."

Emily and I stared at each other open-mouthed at this realisation.

"But which one?" I asked. "I mean, we know Josh was close with her. We know Grantley's a womaniser. As is his son, although most lads in their early twenties are. We know something's not right with the money, and Nigel's falsifying accounts. And we've a heap of clues, none of which make sense. Who got Kateryna pregnant? Why was Redcliff Manor's poker on West Cove beach? Why did Kateryna own a Vivienne Westwood dress?"

I covered my face with my hands.

"And," said Emily, "where's Boots' water bowl?"

I glanced up. "Sorry, Emily. Inconvenient though it is, I hardly think a cat's missing water bowl is pertinent to this investigation."

Oscar cleared his throat. "Here's how we narrow it down. Associate each clue with a suspect. Plus, any reason at all they might've had to murder her. Make a list next to each of their circles."

Emily stood and began searching though drawers. "D'you have a ruler, Shiraz?"

"The other day, I would've said no, but we've found a meat cleaver and a magnifying glass, so who knows?"

Emily tugged a chopping board from a kitchen cupboard. "Here. This'll do. I'll draw lines next to each circle so we can list our evidence."

Oscar rubbed his hands together again. "I do love how the team's collaborating. This is better co-operation than I've seen among many detectives."

Emily drew five straight, neat lines alongside each of the circles, while I boiled the kettle and brought everyone another mug of tea. Cadbury followed me around the kitchen and maintained a constant stare on my packet of digestive biscuits.

"What a marvellous incident room this is," said Oscar. "Refreshments and everything."

"Who shall we start with?" I asked.

"Start with Kateryna. Write down anything pertinent."

"Okay. She was a good-looking young refugee who was pregnant. She worked at Redcliff Manor as a stable hand and bookkeeper. She was unhappy to the point of being suicidal."

"Hang on," said Emily. "I can't write that fast. Let me catch up."

Emily wrote: Refugee. Pregnant. Pretty. Manor stable hand/bookkeeper. Suicidal. She looked up at me. "Keep going."

"One brother killed in the war, one brother fighting. Elderly parents."

Emily scribbled. "Anything else?"

"She owned letters from home, study books and a very nice outfit."

"And some chicken." Emily giggled again.

"You'll have to share this chicken story with me sometime," said Oscar.

I shook my head minutely. "Private joke. Okay. That's Kateryna. Ready to move on?"

"What do we know about Josh?" asked Oscar. "I'll start. People, including me, thought he was her boyfriend. I glimpsed them in town together several times, sitting on the beach wall and chatting. But he denied they had that kind of relationship."

Emily wrote: Boyfriend? "They certainly were close. Grantley said he saw them hugging. Okay, what else? He worked as a fisherman with his dad, and he wasn't very bright." She noted these items.

"He loved kids," I said. "You told us about how he helped at the local school. And he denied being the person who got Kateryna pregnant and took a DNA test to prove that statement. That's all I can think of."

Oscar nodded. "There's one important piece of information about Josh you've omitted."

CHAPTER TWENTY-ONE

I stared at the circles and lines on the paper. "I can't think of anything else we know about Josh. We've noted the boyfriend question, his work, and how he loved kids but says he didn't get Kateryna pregnant. What else is there?"

"He apparently took his own life," said Oscar. "We don't know why. That could be the solution to this entire case."

Emily wrote on the line next to Josh's name: Killed himself.

"All right. Let's move on to another suspect," I said. "Grantley Bramhall."

"Nasty man," said Emily. "Undressed us with his eyes as soon as we walked into the manor. And he didn't seem to care that his employee had died, just that it was inconvenient he had no one to look after his horses now."

Oscar tapped the sheet. "Write all that down. It may be important. However, could I caution you against finding someone guilty of a crime because they're not a particularly nice person? We need to discount our personal feelings about him. And about all the suspects."

"He has a naked picture of his wife in his front hall, for goodness' sake." Emily wrote: Misogynist. Callous.

"That's something that might be important," I said. "His wife doesn't live at the manor. She stays in the city. It could be a clue."

Emily wrote: Separated from wife. "He threatened Josh with a gun too," she said.

"Again, caution," Oscar drummed his fingers. "We mustn't put two and two together and make five. Write down 'owns a gun' for the moment."

"Grantley craves social status to go with his wealth. He wants his son to marry the daughter of the local MP."

"Park that thought for a moment," said Oscar. "We'll connect the dots between the suspects during the next part of the exercise. Write that somewhere else, Emily. Let's move onto our next suspect."

"Nigel." I wrinkled my nose. "Disgusting, snivelling little rat."

"No personal bias, Shiraz," Oscar wagged his finger. "Just the facts. What information do we have about him?"

"He's a cheat. He falsifies Redcliff Manor's accounts."

"Do we know that definitely? It could be Grantley."

"Mrs Kilpatrick told me, Nigel said he always had to correct Kateryna's mistakes. But from what I saw, her bookkeeping was perfect. The reason he was working on the accounts was to cheat. Pure and simple."

Emily wrote: Cheat. False accounting. "And," she added, "he's tight-fisted. When we arrived, collecting for Marine Rescue, he gave us one coin, which we subsequently discovered was a copper one."

"Your picture certainly describes a man who's overly careful with money. Is that all we know about him?"

"He tried to warn me off," I said. "I bumped into him in Emily's café the day after we'd been to Redcliff Manor the second time. He said Mrs Kilpatrick had told him we were asking questions about Kateryna, and he insinuated I should stay away and focus on saving lives at sea."

"Did he just?" asked Oscar. "I wonder what his motives were to say that? Okay, next suspect."

"Joan Kilpatrick. The housekeeper. Although she's eighty years old. She wouldn't be physically capable of killing a young, fit girl and throwing her off a cliff."

"Ooh, I don't know," said Oscar. "I'm seventy, and I can still do thirty push-ups. And I swim in the sea every day of the year with the Redcliff Icebergers."

I laughed. "You're the exception, Oscar. I've never met such a fit septuagenarian. You're an inspiration. Anyway, Mrs Kilpatrick."

"She's very knowledgeable about old paintings," said Emily. "And she's lived at the manor all her life. She's widowed, and her husband used to be a marine rescue volunteer."

"I remember him," said Oscar. "When I was starting out as a trainee, he was an elderly man; no longer an operational member. He must've been considerably older than she was."

I tapped the table. "What's much more relevant about Mrs Kilpatrick is that she said she knew who the father of Kateryna's baby was. How can we go back to the manor for a third time and ask her?"

"We'll work on plans coming out of this session once we've written everything down," said Oscar.

Emily jotted notes about Mrs Kilpatrick.

"Last primary suspect," I said. "Charlie Bramhall. Here's what we know about him. He lives the high life in the city off his father's cash, drives an expensive car and has a string of very young girlfriends. We saw him arrive with one as we were leaving Redcliff Manor on Friday night."

"She looked about eighteen," said Emily. "Long, blonde hair and a little black dress completely unsuited for winter weather."

Emily wrote down facts about Charlie.

"I didn't gather the pair of them were planning on hill walking," I said. "I reckon that dress wasn't staying on very long." I flitted my eyes across the sheet of paper, which looked very organised. "That's all the primary suspects. Now for the secondary ones."

Emily drew straight lines along the chopping board next to Elizabeth Bramhall, Peter Rawlings and Alexandra Flaxworth-Mills.

"First secondary suspect," I said. "Elizabeth Bramhall. What do we know about her?"

"Doesn't live with her husband," said Emily. "What an odd arrangement. If I ever manage to find a man, I won't let him out of my sight."

"I understand she prefers life in the city, and he likes playing country squire. We also know she serves on the board of charities, such as the one that brought Kateryna to Redcliff-upon-Sea."

"Maybe Kateryna uncovered some terrible secret about Mrs Bramhall's family," said Emily, "so Mrs Bramhall arranged to have her murdered? Case closed."

"Emily, that may well be what happened," said Oscar, "but it's certainly one of the more far-fetched theories. Let's concentrate on more likely outcomes for now. As I mentioned, the chances are, someone on this page is your murderer. And we haven't written 'Hit-man' in a circle.

"Okay," I said. "The next secondary suspect. Peter Rawlings. What do we know about him?"

"In his sixties," said Oscar. "He's been a trawlerman all his life. He lives in the same cottage he was born in. His mother lived there too, until her death a few years ago."

"Gosh, so there were three generations of the family all living under one roof."

"Yep. Josh grew up living with his father and grandmother. There was a mystery, I remember, about Peter's wife. They separated, maybe twenty years ago? She wasn't from around here, and everyone presumed she'd returned to her hometown. She kept herself to herself, from memory; the grandmother did all the shopping, housework and so on. I'd forgotten about her until this conversation."

"This exercise is great," said Emily. "Jogging memories and uncovering new facts." She wrote next to Peter Rawlings name: Lived with mother. Separated. Bereaved (son).

"We also know Peter Rawlings discovered Josh's suicide letter. The police told me."

Emily wrote: Found suicide note. Then she appended to Josh's text: Left suicide note.

"Finally," I said, "Alexandra Flaxworth-Mills. What do we know about her?"

"Charlie doesn't want to date her. But she seems keen on him. She phones him and tells him she's wearing his favourite underwear, but he's not interested."

"How on earth have you been party to such intimate conversations?" asked Oscar.

"Um, we hid in the bushes when he pulled up outside Redcliff Manor, and we overheard them on the phone."

"Gosh. You two are enacting stakeouts. Very impressive."

"And we discovered two other things about Charlie." I held up one finger. "First, he lies to that Alexandra girl to avoid seeing her. We heard him tell her he was in London, when he was right in front of us at Redcliff Manor. And secondly"—I held up a second finger—"he has a brand-new horseshoe which he dropped."

"Had a brand-new horseshoe. We took it with us, remember?"

"I forgot we did that. Which coat was I wearing?"

"The long, black one."

Rummaging in the coat's inside pocket revealed the horseshoe, which I laid on the table.

"That's definitely never been on a horse," said Emily. "It's sparkling."

At that moment, Murph entered the kitchen. "All done. New pane of glass in." He glanced at the table. "What are you three drawing? It looks like some complicated design for a town with loads of roundabouts."

"That's what I said." Emily giggled.

"Nothing important, Murph." I tried to hide the diagram. "Just, um, playing a game. What are we learning at training tonight?"

"Bring your best concentration, ladies. In view of your recent unscheduled boat ride, tonight we'll learn tide times and other local hazards."

"See you later, Murph. Thanks so much for fitting the window."

I closed the door behind him, nipped into the living room to inspect his work and collected the horseshoe that had caused the broken window in the first place.

Side by side on the kitchen table, the two horseshoes were identically brand-new and shiny.

Oscar weighed one of the shoes in his hand. "This isn't like any horseshoe I've seen before. I'm not a horse fancier myself, but these are too light. It's like they're made of a different metal. D'you mind if I take one with me and ask someone about it?"

"Of course. Clearly, they're an important clue, so we want to know as much about them as possible."

Emily wrote below her other facts about Charlie: Lies to Alexandra. Has horseshoe in pocket.

"Back to Alexandra," I said. "What else do we know about her, apart from her liking Charlie?"

"She's around twenty-eight, twenty-nine?" said Oscar. "She attended some posh boarding school for girls, but, like Charlie, I don't think she's ever made a career for herself. I've no idea what she does."

"Where does she live?"

"In a large farmhouse near the neighbouring town of Alnchurch. Maybe ten miles up the road past the manor. The family owns around one thousand acres, but they don't farm it. They have some other kind of operation."

Emily wrote next to Alexandra's circle: Late twenties. Lives in farmhouse. Likes Charlie. Unemployed?

"The family's wealthy," continued Oscar. "Her father, the MP; he's old money. His father was also in parliament, and I think his grandfather was too. This is the dynasty Grantley would love to be a member of, even if only by marriage."

"It sounds like his efforts to bring Charlie and Alexandra together'll be an uphill struggle," I said. "If Alexandra's aged in her late twenties, she's about five years older than Charlie."

"And about ten years older than any of his current squeezes." Emily puffed.

"Yep," said Oscar. "This is the exact opposite of *Romeo and Juliet*. The families want the boy and girl to be together, but the couple in question aren't keen."

"One of them seems very keen," said Emily. She replaced the tops on the pens.

"What's next?" I asked. "We've all our suspects in circles, we've noted who's a primary suspect and who's a secondary suspect, and we've written down what we know about each one."

"Next," said Oscar, "let's give each suspect a score out of ten as to how likely they are to be the murderer."

Emily pulled the top off the red pen. "Josh gets a high score. We know him and Kateryna were close. The police believe he killed her. He denied they were a couple, maybe to throw them off the scent."

"When I went for my walk up to the clifftop and played out the scenarios," I said, "I surmised that Josh was the father, he didn't want to keep the baby and Kateryna did. So he killed her to prevent the birth."

"Unlikely," said Oscar. "Look at what we've written about Josh. He took a DNA test to prove he wasn't the father. Even though the results aren't back, he wouldn't have done that unless he was sure. And we know he loved kids. I'm sure he would've been delighted to have a child of his own. I say give him six out of ten, purely because he was closest to Kateryna. Most murders are committed by someone very near to the deceased."

Emily wrote 6/10 next to Josh's name.

"Grantley Bramhall." I tapped the paper. "Employer. Good-looking older man. We know he likes the ladies."

"Ugh." Emily shuddered. "Makes my skin crawl to think about him."

"I theorised they might've had an affair, the baby was Grantley's, and he killed Kateryna as the child would be competition for Charlie's inheritance."

"That's something I hadn't considered," said Oscar. "That's a very possible scenario. I reckon Grantley gets eight out of ten."

Emily wrote 8/10 next to Grantley's name.

"Nigel," I said. "The theory I keep coming back to is, Kateryna threatened to expose his creative accounting. He may've been siphoning off Grantley's money somehow."

"A flimsy guess," said Oscar. "We know something was wrong with the accounts but, as the bookkeeper, Kateryna could've been in on the scheme. She might've benefited from it too."

"Plus," said Emily, "I can't believe Nigel's physically capable of killing Kateryna. We know she was young and fit. Shiraz, you told me she raced up the cliff path despite being pregnant. And Nigel's a little weed."

"Give him five," said Oscar.

"Who's next?" I asked. "Mrs Kilpatrick."

"She didn't kill Kateryna." Emily shook her head. "She's over eighty. And she seems so nice."

"I agree," said Oscar. "If the cause of death had been poisoning or something, maybe. But Kateryna met a violent, physical end. Give Mrs Kilpatrick one out of ten."

"Charlie Bramhall?" I said. "Kateryna would've been at the upper end of his preferred age-range. Look at the posh teenager we saw getting out of his car the other night. Kateryna was the exact opposite of her. She was a refugee stable hand. Plus, Charlie didn't live at the manor. We know he only came down to show off his country estate to his girlfriends. Charlie seems more likely than Mrs Kilpatrick, I suppose, but less likely than the others."

"Okay, we'll give him four," said Emily.

"Now, the secondary suspects," said Oscar. "Peter Rawlings."

"Nought out of ten," I said. "I can't see any motive at all."

"We don't give anyone nought at this stage," said Oscar.

"Oooh," said Emily. "Maybe Peter Rawlings is the father?"

"That's a far-fetched scenario," said Oscar. "Peter's sixty-odd years old, but he's had a hard, outdoor life and looks ten years older. And I recall he only has one hand. When he was a child, he found an unexploded World War II grenade on the beach, picked it up and it blew his hand off. Gosh, he is going to find it hard not having Josh's help on the boat. Anyway, my point is, a young lady might not find him attractive."

"Three out of ten," I said. "Next, Elizabeth Bramhall. She can't have a score of any more than one. She doesn't even come to Redcliff. We could almost rule her out."

"Okay. Write down one out of ten for now," said Oscar. "And lastly, Alexandra Flaxworth-Mills."

"She's not connected with Kateryna. She has a loose line to Charlie."

"That line must've been stronger once," said Emily.

I frowned. "How d'you know that?"

"The underwear conversation. At some point, he's seen her in her underwear."

"Gosh, yes, you're right. You're a great detective. At the very least, they had a brief affair. But that has nothing to do with Kateryna."

"I'm giving her one out of ten as well," said Emily. "There's no motive I can see."

I sat back and stared at the paper, covered with circles, lines, text and now mathematical equations.

"The last thing to do," said Oscar, "is note down the clues which don't seem connected with anything else, together with any details we know about them."

Emily chose another pen and wrote: Poker. Found on West Cove. May come from Redcliff Manor hall.

"The horseshoes," I prompted. "They could be a very important clue. I noticed one was missing from above the stable doors at Redcliff Manor."

Emily wrote: Horseshoe. May come from Redcliff Manor stables.

"And the note about Jerusalem," said Oscar. "That may've been inserted while the money box was left in Redcliff Manor kitchen."

Emily wrote: Jerusalem note. May come from Redcliff Manor kitchen.

"I'm starting to see a common factor with these clues," I said. "Oscar, if you were back in your investigating days, what would you do now?"

"This is where the fun really starts." He rubbed his hands together. "We gather evidence which either increases or decreases those figures out of ten until we have a clear suspect. For instance, if we discovered one of our primary suspects had a verifiable alibi, their number would drop. If we unearthed new evidence which put a low-numbered suspect in the vicinity at the time of the murder, their number would increase."

"But where do we start?" I shook my head.

"I have a suggestion," said Oscar. "Kill two birds with one stone, if you'll pardon the expression. Visit Peter Rawlings and ask him about Josh. Then, you'll be able to adjust your scores for both of them."

"Hmm," I said. "What excuse could we use for popping in?"

"We could take him flowers by way of condolence," suggested Emily. "We'll say they're from the team at Redcliff Marine Rescue."

"Marine Rescue! What time is it?" I jumped up, which prompted Cadbury to leap to his feet and bark. "Emily, we need to go. We're late for training."

CHAPTER TWENTY-TWO

"Good evening, everyone," boomed Murph at our group of five trainees. "I was going to talk to you tonight about the drills we rehearse on the vessel, such as fire on board or abandon ship but, as some of you appear to need additional instruction in interpreting tides and local hazards, we'll kick off with those."

My cheeks reddened. Emily nudged me and giggled.

"As two of you learnt last night, the tides at Headland Bay are different to the tides at Redcliff." He passed around small, white booklets with blue writing. "These are tide tables. They're also freely available on the Internet, and I seem to remember Emily has a larger version of this book pinned to her café wall."

Emily looked serious and whispered, "*That* is particularly embarrassing."

Murph held page one of his copy open and faced it to us with his forefinger on the left-hand page. "You'll notice here it states the difference in tide times at various landmarks, when compared to Headland Bay. Redcliff,"—he stared at

Emily and me—"including West Cove, is twenty minutes different from Headland Bay."

"So high tide"—he again looked our way—"is twenty minutes earlier. Whereas the tide at Arthur's Reef is thirty minutes earlier than Headland Bay, and at Blakey's Island it's only fifteen. Remember this when you're planning a voyage, or"—he stared at us again—"a walk."

"Do you feel you're being picked on?" whispered Emily.

"At least he's not naming and shaming."

"Now, other local hazards." Murph set the small book down and pointed at a chart on the wall behind him. "Arthur's Reef, where the tide is, how many minutes earlier than Headland Bay, Shiraz?"

"Thirty," I said confidently.

"Good to see you're listening. Arthur's Reef is a shallow area roughly ten nautical miles offshore. Most small vessels can navigate it without incident but, at low spring tides, there may be around two feet of water there, and several boats have run aground over the years. People who don't know the local hazards, like we do."

Murph's presentation continued, and I listened intently. The last thing I wanted to be was the person who ran the rescue boat up on the rocks.

The plain, green, wooden door to Peter Rawlings' cottage was ajar. I knocked and stooped slightly in the doorway. Emily followed me into a living room with low, black, ceiling beams.

Late-afternoon gloom shone through a small window in the far wall which barely increased the visibility inside. Through a rear door, a kitchen with a bare, flagstone floor contained a deep, stone sink. Burning wood glowed bright orange in a fireplace and, in the corner of the room, seated in a tattered armchair, an old man held a photograph in his left hand.

If this was Peter Rawlings, he looked eighty, not sixty. Maybe Oscar had his age wrong?

I brandished the flowers in front of me. "Mr Rawlings? I'm Shiraz; this is Emily. We're from Redcliff Marine Rescue."

The man glanced up but didn't engage with my eyes. He nodded once.

"We've come to offer our sincere condolences on the tragic loss of your son."

The man gestured we should sit on a threadbare sofa which struggled to stay level. I plopped into one end of it, and my backside was immediately engulfed by broken springs. Emily perched on the opposite arm.

The man pointed at the mantelpiece above the fire, where a vase stood containing blooms which had drunk all their water and given up being attractive.

"Would you like me to replace these for you?" asked Emily.

He nodded twice, then returned his gaze to the photo in his hand. Emily stood and lifted the vase. She took the new flowers from me and carried them both into the back room. I heard a tap run.

"Mr Rawlings? Is that a photo of Josh you're holding?"

He nodded again. I stood with some difficulty as a 'boi-oi-oing' sounded from beneath me. He turned the photo towards me, and I crouched to see it more closely.

My forefinger and thumb held the right hand of the photo, and I expected the man to release his side, but he gripped the photo strongly, so we held it between us. Emily returned with the fresh flowers in the vase and placed it back on the mantelpiece.

"He was a good-looking lad," I said.

Peter Rawlings looked up at me. No tears moistened his eyes, but his face remained in a constant frown. He nodded twice again. I wondered if he'd left the chair in the last two days.

I put my arm on his shoulder, which was covered in a moth-eaten jumper, and squeezed gently. "Would you like to tell me about him?"

Mr Rawlings returned his gaze to the photo. I glanced at his right arm resting on the chair. The end of the jumper's sleeve had been tied in a knot, so his missing right hand was concealed.

234

This man's lost two right hands. The one on his body, and his son.

"He wasn't a clever boy."

I jumped, as the deep, country burr of Mr Rawlings' voice sounded for the first time. Slow and steady.

"But he was loyal and reliable." Mr Rawlings bit his bottom lip so hard with his three yellow top teeth it turned white.

"I can't understand why they arrested him. And now he's gone, and I'll never know." He sobbed once, but still no tears came. He thumped the chair's arm with his stump. "That's what makes me so angry. He was such a caring, gentle lad. He loved nothing more than to care for others, whether it was fetching me my tea, or entertaining kids at the school, or back in the day, sitting at Molly's bedside."

He tugged the photo from my grip, slumped back in his chair and ground his teeth.

"Who's Molly, Mr Rawlings?"

Peter Rawlings pushed himself forward and pointed to a small table next to the sofa. A framed photo stood on it. I reached over, picked it up and turned it around. It was black and white and contained two figures.

The left-hand one was Josh, grinning, holding a fish almost as big as himself.

The right-hand one was a face I'd seen before.

A girl, maybe the same age as Josh, with her arm around him.

The right-hand figure was the girl inside the locket.

CHAPTER TWENTY-THREE

I gasped.

"What's wrong?" asked Emily.

"Emily, quick. Which coat was I wearing on Sunday?"

"How on earth would I know? I can't remember what I wore yesterday, let alone what you wore on Sunday. What were we doing on Sunday?"

My words spewed out like a machine gun. "West Cove. Dark. Cold. Saved by Redcliff Marine Rescue." I patted my pockets, unzipped my jacket and stuffed my hands in the inner lining. In the bottom corner of the left-hand pocket, something small responded to my fingers.

"Got it." I tugged out the locket. "Mr Rawlings, d'you recognise this?" I held it up to his face, probably too closely, and he recoiled and peered at it.

"That belonged to Josh." He took it from me. "He always wore it around his neck. Where did you find it?"

"On West Cove beach. On Sunday. Emily and I were, um, taking a walk, and she saw it glistening among the rocks."

He couldn't open it with his one hand, so I took it back again and unclipped the latch. I held the picture inside the locket up against the photo in the frame. Unquestionably, they were the same girl.

"He loved her so much," said Peter. I couldn't believe it was possible for someone to appear even sadder than he had a few minutes ago, but now he did. Silent tears ran down his cheeks, and I realised I'd never seen an older man cry.

"Emily," I hissed. "Tissues."

She nipped into the rear kitchen to find something for Mr Rawlings to wipe his tears away.

"Who is she, Peter?" I asked.

"Molly. Josh's twin sister. She died in a car crash three years ago."

He paused as grief obstructed his words. Emily returned and dabbed his face gently. I idly thought she'd have made a very good nurse, or carer. She crouched on the opposite side of him from me, as he haltingly told his story.

"Like Josh, she wasn't a clever girl. She loved animals and nature. She volunteered at Redcliff Horse Sanctuary."

He paused again, gazed at his woollen, holey socks then glanced up.

"Josh wouldn't leave her side. He held her hand at the hospital until..."

That sentence didn't get finished, but it didn't need to.

"I couldn't leave the fishing boat; it was our only source of income. To be honest, it was probably an escape from the situation at home." His chin dipped down to his chest.

"My wife, she'd left decades ago. She didn't enjoy life in Redcliff and missed her family. My mother passed away, and once Molly died, it was just Josh and me."

He exhaled deeply and shook his head. Emily wiped his face with another tissue.

I went in for a direct hit. Surely this man couldn't become any sadder.

"Mr Rawlings, why d'you think Josh took his own life?"

He turned and stared at me, as if this was the first time he'd heard he'd lost both his children.

"This girl, Katherine, we called her. She had a foreign name, but it sounded like Katherine."

Yes! This is where we discover everything and solve the murder.

"Josh walked alone on the cliffs. He said it reminded him of Molly, and how she loved the natural world. He met Katherine up there, alone in their thoughts and together at the same time. Like destiny. Katherine explained how she used to walk there and talk to her dead brother. Josh said the same about Molly. The two of them filled a gap in each other's lives. Neither of them had ever been able to grieve properly." He waved his arm in the air expressively. "When Katherine died, it was like he'd lost Molly all over again."

239

"Were you surprised when he was arrested?" asked Emily.

I glared at her, then realised she could've asked a crucial question.

"Of course. The poor boy was worried sick. Katherine was supposed to meet him at the boat after we returned from fishing, but she never showed up. He was about to go looking for her, up on the cliffs in the dark. I told him not to; he might end up walking over the edge. Then we heard Redcliff Marine Rescue had found her body."

"Wait," I said. "Are you telling me Josh was fishing with you when she was murdered?"

"He was." Mr Rawlings thumped the arm of the chair with his stump. "I told the police. But they wouldn't accept my statement. They said I was protecting my son. They'd made up their minds about him already." He dropped the locket into his lap and rubbed his face with his hand. "He took his own life so he could be with Molly, and with Katherine."

A knock at the door, then a woman entered carrying a dish of food. "Sorry, Peter. I didn't realise you had company."

Emily and I stood. "It's okay. We were leaving."

"I'm the next-door neighbour," she explained. "I pop in regularly to check on him. Isn't this whole thing so awful?"

My mouth straightened, and I nodded, turned to Peter again, bent down and hugged him. I wanted to say, "Sorry for your loss," or "I hope you feel better soon," but how could any words help this man who'd now lost both his children?

Emily exhaled hard as we strolled away from Peter Rawlings' little cottage. "I need a cup of tea after that. How can one family suffer so much tragedy? It's not fair."

"Come back to my place. Let's review our incident sheet. Based on that conversation, I'm inclined to downgrade Josh's score."

"Yes." Emily nodded. "Not only did he love kids, it seems that Kateryna and him had a brother and sister relationship. Plus, Peter Rawlings says Josh was fishing with him at the time of the murder."

The giant piece of paper remained spread over the entire table.

"Where do you eat?" asked Emily.

"I had breakfast standing up this morning. The last thing I want to do is spill coffee over our investigation sheet."

241

"Especially not a takeaway from my café." Emily picked up the packet of pens. "Josh was a six out of ten. What shall we make him now?"

"A two. And change Peter Rawlings from a three to a one. Who shall we visit next?"

"We've had an initial chat with everyone, except Elizabeth Bramhall and this Alexandra girl."

"Who's our top suspect?" My eyes darted around the giant paper. "It's still Grantley Bramhall, and then Nigel."

"We can hardly waltz back into Redcliff Manor again, can we? We've already been twice, and the second time was a stroke of luck."

"Yep. We'll need to put our heads together. That Nigel chap thinks we're up to something."

"Okay. Let's save that for when we see Oscar next. In the meantime, how about we pay Alexandra a visit? We can rule her out, at the very least."

"What excuse could we give? She lives miles out of town, and we've no reason to drop in on her."

"We still have the money box." Emily picked up the two halves and clipped them back together.

"What, we're touring the entire countryside collecting for Redcliff Marine Rescue, and we'd appreciate her support, even though she doesn't live in Redcliff-upon-Sea and probably has nothing to do with boats."

"D'you have any better ideas? We can take my car."

I shrugged. "So what's your plan? Drive out to the Flaxworth-Mills' farmhouse, toodle up to the front door, hope Alexandra answers, say, 'Hello, we're collecting for Marine Rescue and, by the way, did you happen to murder a stable girl working at Redcliff Manor?' At times like this I wish we'd never become involved with this case."

"We don't have to go," said Emily.

I sighed. "Yes, we do. Because if we don't, a murderer will get away scot-free. All of this"—I waved my hand across the table at the squiggles, lines and circles—"will have been for nothing. Grab your coat. Where's your car parked?"

CHAPTER TWENTY-FOUR

For some reason, I'd assumed Emily's car would be a recent model and large enough to carry all the goods a café might need to procure. Maybe a hatchback where the rear seats could fold down? Or a saloon with a huge boot? Or even a small van?

Nope.

"I know it's a sunny day, Emily, but it's midwinter," I yelled above the noise of the engine and the wind whistling past my ears. "D'you usually have the top down when the air temperature's about eight degrees?"

"I always say," shouted Emily, as her hair flapped across her face to the point where I wondered how she could see to drive, "what's the point in owning a convertible unless you convert it? I cringe if I see a soft-top car with the roof closed on a nice day."

"So how long have you owned this car?" I tossed my fringe back and wished I'd brought a hair tie.

"This Morris Minor is over sixty years old. It belonged to my grandmother. She left it to me when she passed away, as I loved riding in it as a child."

"I've never travelled in a car with no seatbelts." I frantically tried to grab at something as we rounded a sharp bend, possibly on two wheels.

"She pre-dates them," shouted Emily. "Handles well for an old girl, doesn't she? Top speed of 65 miles per hour."

"Very," I said, bracing myself as my body slammed into the passenger door which I hoped wouldn't suddenly open. "Could you turn the heating up?"

"It's as high as it'll go. On really cold days, I bring a hot water bottle."

We swept past the turning to Redcliff Manor, then whizzed by a quaint country pub with white-framed windows and hanging baskets filled with winter blooms. Smoke rose from a chimney, and I wished I were inside by the fire instead of freezing my ears off in Emily's car.

"The King's Arms," said Emily, as the building disappeared over my right shoulder. "It used to be a pub for the farmers around here, but new people took it over and turned it into one of these modern gastropubs with an expensive menu. Goodness knows how much business they do; I know from running the café that the folk around here want basic, filling food. Bacon sandwiches and roast dinners. Not Thai green curry and duck canapes."

A sign advising we'd entered the village of Alnchurch flashed past on my left.

"How far is it to the Flaxworth-Mills' farm?" I asked, wondering whether I'd die of cold before we reached there. My cheeks had turned completely numb, and I'd long since given up on any attempt at a hairstyle.

"We're here." Emily pressed the indicator stalk and swung the wheel into a long, straight driveway, framed by stone pillars supporting a pair of white, five-bar gates. Tall, stout trees bordered the track and horses grazed in paddocks separated by wooden fencing. As we slowed down, my face defrosted and, by the time we pulled up in front of the double-storey farmhouse, I could actually feel my nose.

Emily switched off the engine, and the first thing I noticed was the silence. No vehicles, humans or agricultural noise. The not-unpleasant smell of equine manure permeated the air. I glanced around at the horses, most of which wore coats of differing colours, all with a white logo embroidered on them.

My head swivelled, as the crunch of gravel announced the arrival of a sturdy young woman dressed in a green, waxed jacket, cream-coloured jodhpurs and dark-brown boots.

"I say," she said, pointing at Emily's car, "What a marvellous chariot you have there. How absolutely spiffing."

She marched towards us, removed her riding helmet and shook free a blonde ponytail. "I always say one should drive a good old-fashioned charabanc. None of these flashy, modern things. I own a 1975 Jaguar myself."

She stuck out a hand. "Alexandra Flaxworth-Mills. Part-owner and manager of Flaxworth-Mills Horse Stud. Wonderful to make your acquaintance."

Bingo.

"I'm Emily. Owner of the, erm, chariot. This is my friend, Shiraz."

"Shiraz, hey? How frightfully wonderful. I do love an exotic name. What can I do for both of you?"

Emily began to unlock the car boot to retrieve the collecting box, but I waggled my hand at her.

"We're from Redcliff Marine Rescue," I said, shaking Alexandra's hand professionally. "We'd heard about your successful business, and we wondered whether you'd be interested in sponsoring one of our vessels. We have investment opportunities to suit all budgets, and the exposure that goes with supporting such a high-profile charity would do wonders for your brand."

"What a simply terrific suggestion," said Alexandra. "Do come into the warm and tell me all about it."

She opened the front door and led us inside.

Emily opened her eyes wide and whispered to me, "Where did that come from?"

"I was married to a public relations man, remember?"

"Do sit wherever you like," said our host, as she cleared newspapers and magazines from a sofa and piled them onto the threadbare, room-sized rug.

We plopped beside each other and glanced around the room. "What an establishment you have here," I said. "How many horses d'you own?"

"Oh, are you a horse lover too?"

"No, not really, but..."

"Fabulous. We have fifty horses here, both ours and ones we look after for others. Ten staff, including a head trainer, a consultant jockey and even a vet. Should it be needed, we can treat any horse's illness or injuries right here at the stud. We have the most advanced facility of its type in the country, I believe."

I feigned interest. "Very impressive. I'm sure sponsorship of the rescue boat could only improve your profile in the community."

Alexandra shot a glance at a wooden carriage clock on the mantelpiece. "Tea? Four o'clock. My tum-tum's not going to make it as far as dinner without a little smackerel of something."

"Thank you," I said. "Tea would be lovely on such a cold day."

"Earl Grey, Assam or Lapsang-Souchong?

I glanced at Emily, who stuck her bottom lip out and shrugged.

"Earl Grey, please."

Alexandra nipped into a nearby room, and we heard rattling china.

The clutter in the living room rivalled Grantley Bramhall's study. An antique dresser covered in crockery filled one wall, and a large table which couldn't have been dined upon for years stood in the centre, buried under stacks of papers. Small wood-and-wicker chairs had been scattered around the edges of the room and were similarly concealed under various artefacts.

Emily pointed at the pile of papers Alexandra had relocated to allow us to sit. "Isn't that the same magazine we saw in Kateryna's room?"

"*Red Carpet Superstars*. My old nemesis Victoria Harrington on the cover." I reached forward to pick it up, but at that point Alexandra arrived, carrying a tray.

"Here we are. A pot of Earl Grey tea and home baking." She set the tray down on top of two equal-height piles of papers. "Milk?"

"Yes, please," we both said.

"Sugar?"

"No, thanks." I watched Alexandra drop three lumps into her own cup.

"Cake?" She handed us a small plate each. "There's Victoria sponge, shortbread, lemon slice, ginger cake and melting moments. All home-made by Mummy."

"Thank you." I accepted a slice of sponge, and Emily took a piece of shortbread. I watched as Alexandra placed one of each item on her own plate and ate a melting moment in one bite.

"Tell me about this sponsorship," she said. "I'm all ears." She stuffed the ginger cake in her mouth.

"Um, our boat at Redcliff Marine Rescue's well-known," I said. "It's prominent in the community. In return for a donation, your company's name could be displayed on the side."

"I've even heard of boats being named after their sponsors," said Emily. "Our vessel could become Flaxworth-Mills Horse Stud Marine Rescue."

Goodness knows how we're going to sell this to Murph if she says yes.

"That all sounds jolly wonderful. How much would you want us to give?" The lemon slice disappeared between her lips, closely followed by the shortbread.

I waved the back of one hand. "We'll work out the finer details later. We just wanted to see if you'd be interested, as one of the more important businesses in the area."

"I'll have to discuss this with Daddy; he's the other partner, but I'm sure we'd love to help." She rammed the sponge in with the heel of her palm.

A grandfather clock chimed behind us, and I jumped.

"Gracious me, is that the time?" exclaimed Alexandra. "Awfully sorry, I must feed out hay before it's pitch black out there. Do excuse me. I'll be in touch." She stood and grabbed a further piece of ginger cake.

I tipped back my tea. "We quite understand. Thank you so much for the tea and baking. Delicious."

"I must ask Mummy to top up the cake supplies. We seem to be running low. I'll need some to take to a tea party on Thursday at Redcliff Manor."

We followed her through the front door.

"Goodbye. Wonderful of you to drop in." She pointed at the Morris Minor. "Fabulous chariot. Absolutely fabulous."

"Emily, must we have the top down continually?" I asked, as we bumped along the drive. "It's not only cold, but now it's getting dark as well. If I'd known, I would've brought a hat."

Emily slapped her forehead. "Hat. I have two in the boot. Hold on." She stopped the car, nipped out and returned with two woollen beanies. "Here. Now you'll be warmer."

I pulled the hat over my ears as we turned into the main road, and the car's dim headlights lit up the verge.

"What did we learn from that visit?" asked Emily.

"Nothing. I can't see how in any way she could be connected with Kateryna's murder. Although I can see why Charlie Bramhall doesn't want to go along with his father's arranged marriage plans. She's very overbearing. The tea was delicious, though. I always say it tastes better out of a pot."

"Me too. But it's gone right through me. I'll pop in here to use the loo." She swerved the wheel to the left, and we pulled into the driveway of the King's Arms.

"D'you need to go?" she asked.

"No, but I'll come inside and wait for you. It's too cold sitting in the car."

We entered the pub, and Emily followed signs to the toilets. I leant against a low desk inside the door and looked around the dining room. Tables covered in white linen and laid with cutlery were scattered throughout, but none were occupied.

Behind the desk, a board on an easel had been propped out of the way.

A glance at it revealed a seating plan for a function, such as a wedding. Emily hadn't reappeared, so I idly studied the names assigned to the tables.

I paused, as I identified several I recognised.

CHAPTER TWENTY-FIVE

"Emily. Look at this."

She gazed over my shoulder at the sign board. "Standard wedding catering," she said. "Chicken or beef. Swap plates with the person next to you if you don't enjoy yours."

"I don't mean the menu. This is a seating plan for an event hosted by Sir James Flaxworth-Mills. 7:00 p.m. Charity fundraiser for the Home for Retired Jockeys. Look at the names on it."

She peered closer. "The top table has Sir James Flaxworth-Mills and Lady Charlotte Flaxworth-Mills, together with other titled people."

"Yep. That's not surprising, considering who organised the dinner. But look closer at table three." I tapped on the circle with a '3' in the centre.

"Eight people. Oh. Including Grantley Bramhall and Charlie Bramhall."

"Look who's sitting on the other side of Charlie."

"Nigel Whitmore. Is that Grantley's personal assistant?"

"Yes. Mrs Kilpatrick told us his full name, when she was explaining he had to correct Kateryna's accounting."

"Before I was forced to inspect paintings of fat men in shooting gear."

We heard footsteps behind us, and a middle-aged man approached wearing a smart, grey apron with 'The King's Arms' embroidered on it in white, cursive writing.

"Sorry, I didn't hear you come in," he said. "Were you wanting dinner tonight? The kitchen's just opening."

"We, um, were considering booking at some point. I did have one question for you."

"Certainly? Did you want to ask about the menu? We offer several vegetarian and vegan options."

"No. This may seem a strange request but, when was this dinner held?" I pointed at the seating plan.

"Ah, Sir James's function. A very prestigious affair. We had to employ extra waiting staff." He flicked backwards through a hardback diary lying on the desk and ran his finger down one of the pages. "It was two Fridays ago. Wonderful occasion. Three hours of dinner, drinks and speeches. If only we could host more events like that, we'd be doing well. There's nothing else of that size booked until a wedding at Easter."

"Thank you," I said. "You've been most helpful. We'll come back for dinner one day, won't we, Emily?"

"Definitely." She held the door open for me.

"You realise what this means?" I shouted, as Emily pulled out of the pub's car park and roared down the road towards Redcliff-upon-Sea. At least my hair was staying in place under the beanie.

"What does it mean? Sir James doesn't think Grantley's good enough for his top table?" She laughed. "That's one in the eye for his arranged marriage scheme."

"No, silly. The date of that event was the same as the night Kateryna died."

"Gosh. What a coincidence. That was a busy night. It's a good job Murph wasn't invited. His pager would've gone off in the middle of the speeches."

"Don't you get it? This puts our investigation back to the start."

"It does?"

"Of course. This event means our three top suspects have a cast-iron alibi."

"Goodness, you're right. Now what do we do?"

"D'you want to come up?" asked Emily, as she locked the Morris Minor in its garage behind the café.

"I'll walk home, thanks. I need a hot bath."

"Okay. See you tomorrow morning? Pop in for coffee."

"Yep. See you."

I strode along the seafront with my head down and my hands in my pockets. Waves crashed against the sea wall, and an icy breeze whistled across the esplanade.

No one else was crazy enough to be out on an evening like this.

I wrapped my arms around myself, pulled my lapels up and realised I'd forgotten to return Emily's beanie, which was a good job as it still kept my head warm.

My fingers fumbled with the key, and I let myself into Melville Cottage. The heating must've been on a timer, as the warmth began to defrost my cheeks. I ran upstairs to the bathroom and turned on the taps, poured a small bottle of body wash into the tub and watched the bubbles swirl and build little frothy mountains in the ocean of suds.

While the water flowed into the bath, I nipped downstairs, boiled the kettle and made a cup of hibiscus tea. This wasn't my preferred flavour, but a selection of teabags I'd never normally buy had been left in the accommodation, so I thought I'd try something different.

I glanced at the incident sheet covering the dining table and its circles, squiggles and lines. Following our discoveries, it would need a lot of updating. Tomorrow.

I found two candles and a box of matches in the drawer that had contained the magnifying glass and string, so I set them on two saucers, carried them upstairs, placed them strategically at the head and the foot of the bath and lit them. The Spotify app on my phone provided rainforest background music. I undressed, switched out the lights, slipped under the bubbles, which threatened to overflow the edge of the tub, lay back and breathed slowly.

I thought of Kateryna, her pretty, frightened face. Josh, at rest with his sister. Terrible tragedies in this town of terrible tragedies.

Nobody had murdered Kateryna.

Everybody had either been elsewhere at her time of death, or for one or other reason couldn't have killed her.

Maybe she'd committed suicide after all, and the death by blunt trauma diagnosis was a mistake?

I knew I was missing something.

So many loose ends.

Why was the poker on West Cove? Who'd thrown a horseshoe through my window, and why?

I rubbed my eyes.

Why did Kateryna have those beautiful clothes?

And what did the message in the money box mean, and who had put it there?

Maybe there were innocent explanations.

One of the candles extinguished in a breeze from the ill-fitting bathroom window.

I reflected over the ten days—*was it only ten days?*—since I'd arrived back in Redcliff.

I'd made two good friends. Emily was a soulmate, probably the most genuine friend I'd ever had, and I knew I could count on her. I never thought I'd be friends with a seventy-year-old man, but Oscar was such a good conversationalist, advisor, mentor, I thought of him as being my age.

And then there was David. Him of the beautiful eyes, the warm smile, the knowledgeable, modest personality. What was I going to do about him? I hugged myself and grinned.

My marine rescue training was going well. I'd learnt so much in three academic evenings and one turn on the boat. Two turns, if you counted Emily and my unscheduled night duty. Murph was a good teacher, and I respected his experience.

One thing I was definite about.

I'd made the right decision to leave my old, vapid London life behind.

Finally, I was making a difference.

Finally, I was being me.

I just needed to get this unplanned detective distraction out of the way, and I could continue living my new life.

Unlike Kateryna. And Josh. And Molly.

I closed my eyes, as the rainforest music soothed me, and the candle flickered shadows across the ceiling.

CHAPTER TWENTY-SIX

I stood with my arms outstretched leaning forwards on my kitchen table. Oscar sipped a mug of tea. Cadbury lay at his feet and inspected us, lifting one eyebrow at a time. Emily sat back in her chair and gazed at me expectantly.

I thumped the table. "Team. The reason I've gathered you here today is..."

"Woah, woah, woah." Emily held up her palms. "I appreciate you're fired up and ready to go, but I've been up since 5:00 a.m., we have first aid training tonight, and I need an afternoon nap. Could you please not speak to us like you're addressing a board meeting?"

"Sorry, sorry." I pulled out a chair and sat, so at least we were all at the same level.

"I thought you sounded very professional," said Oscar. "What d'you have to tell us?"

"We need a restart. New information has come to light which rules out many former suspects."

"Ah, yes," said Oscar. "I heard you visited Peter Rawlings. Poor chap. How did you get on?"

"He's innocent, and so is his son. Josh and Kateryna had a platonic brother and sister-type relationship. They'd both been bereaved of their own siblings, and they filled a gap in each other's lives. Josh must've been devastated when Kateryna died."

"Indeed," said Oscar. "I recall his sister's accident now. Tragic. Okay, so you've revised your scores for Peter and Josh Rawlings?"

I slid the pens over to Emily. "Would you be scribe again?"

"Of course." She opened the packet and pulled out the red marker.

"We've dropped Josh and Peter's scores to two and one respectively," I said. "I'd happily drop them to zero, but you counselled not to do that."

Oscar nodded. "Correct; not yet. What else did you find out?"

"We took a trip to the Flaxworth-Mills' horse stud. Emily drove me in her convertible Morris Minor." I winked at her. "She nearly froze me to death."

Emily poked out her bottom lip. "You won't be saying that when we're heading off for a picnic together on a summer's day."

I rubbed her shoulder. "I can't wait for all this to be over so we can do that."

"Did you manage to see Alexandra?" Oscar craned his neck across the sheet. "You gave her one out of ten before."

"Yep, we saw her, but we didn't gain any information that increased that score."

"She liked my car," said Emily. "I'm glad someone does."

"Emily," I said. "I love convertibles. Just not in mid-January."

"Apart from liking your car," asked Oscar, "did she impart any other useful information?"

"Not really. I fabricated a story on the spur of the moment about her horse stud business sponsoring a marine rescue boat. I've no idea if that kind of thing actually happens. Anyway, it gave us an excuse to go inside and talk to her. All we found out was that her house is full of antiques and newspapers, and her mother's a great home baker. I can't see any motive, or any connection Alexandra would've had with Kateryna."

Emily leant forward. "Can you believe she ate five cakes while we were there? I reckon she must have an afternoon tea that size every day. She'll never be a racing jockey, that's for certain."

"Racing jockey." Oscar pulled one of the horseshoes from his pocket. "That reminds me. I asked a friend about this horseshoe. He said it's unusual, because it's made of a light alloy, not the heavy metal that most shoes are made from. He told me it'd be used for shoeing racing thoroughbreds."

"Does that help us at all?" said Emily. "We found one of them on Redcliff Manor's drive next to Charlie's car, and the three horses Kateryna cared for definitely weren't thoroughbreds. More like old nags."

"Here's the biggest piece of information from the day," I said. "On the way back from the Flaxworth-Mills' farm, we stopped at a pub called the King's Arms."

"Did you have dinner there?" asked Oscar. "Last I heard, that place had gone all upmarket, with white linen tables and an expensive menu. People around here mainly want good, honest, old-fashioned pub meals. I'm not sure how long it'll last."

"You're right," said Emily. "Nobody was dining. We only popped in to use the toilet."

"And to defrost my face."

"And to defrost Shiraz's face."

"And what did you discover there?" asked Oscar, "while you were defrosting your face?"

"A very important piece of information. The same night Kateryna was murdered, Grantley Bramhall, Charlie Bramhall and Nigel were all at a function there. That's our top three suspects in the clear."

Oscar pursed his lips. "Can you be sure they were at the event exactly at the same time she was murdered?"

"The seating plan said the dinner started at 7:00 p.m. Then the man at the pub told us it went on for three hours of dinner, drinks and speeches. I remember, I saw the rescue boat go out well after dark that night, although I can't recall the exact time."

"Assuming the alibi for all of them stacks up," said Oscar, "where does that leave us?"

"If we reduce all of their scores to one out of ten," said Emily, "then everybody has a score of one. Except Josh, and he should probably be a one as well."

"We're back on an even playing field," said Oscar. "All the suspects are still just as guilty as each other. Either we need to consider someone new who we haven't thought about, or we've missed an important clue."

I held my head in my hands and stared at the paper. Emily leant back and replaced the cap on the pen. Cadbury snuffled and turned over in his sleep.

"If I might make a suggestion?" said Oscar.

"Of course." I nodded. "Any plan's better than no plan."

"You'll have to return to Redcliff Manor. The home of the victim, the home of several suspects and, if I may coin a phrase, ground zero. Grantley Bramhall was your number one suspect. Maybe inquire as to how long he remained at that dinner? Then ask him straight out if anyone at the house had any kind of relationship with Kateryna? Including him. Let slip you know somebody did. It's an old police interrogation trick. Tell a suspect something you know, in this case that he was a guest at the dinner, then ask him something you don't know. Often criminals crack and spill the beans if they think you've worked out their secrets."

"I agree," said Emily. "And we could ask Mrs Kilpatrick to finish her statement about who the father of Kateryna's baby was."

"Gosh, yes. Those two conversations might well clear up this whole mystery. How are we going to enter the house again? We can hardly waltz in brandishing the collection tin a third time. Which reminds me, I still haven't returned it to Murph."

"You could use the same ruse you employed at the Flaxworth-Mills?" suggested Oscar. "Grantley Bramhall's made a lot of money in his life. Ask him if he'd sponsor a boat?"

I laid my hand on his arm. "Oscar, what would we do without you?"

"We three make a great team," said Emily. "Maybe we could go to Redcliff Manor tomorrow? Let's meet at the café at closing time and finalise plans. Two o'clock in the afternoon."

CHAPTER TWENTY-SEVEN

"Good evening, everyone. Welcome to tonight's first aid course, a requirement for every crew member."

Murph was in full voice standing at the front of the marine rescue training room, although his laptop was winning the technology battle, and David helped him display his presentation.

"For you five new members,"—he swept his finger around the right side of the room, where Emily and I sat with three other new recruits—"I believe this is the first time you've learnt first aid. Have any of you completed a qualification at work, or as part of other volunteering?"

We all indicated we hadn't.

"Everybody else who's taking part in their annual recertification;"—he nodded at the left-hand side of the room, where David sat with four other crew members I hadn't met before—"you're experts who hopefully haven't forgotten anything since last year. So tonight, for the practical, we'll buddy up each qualified crew member with a newbie."

I glanced at the back of David's head and willed him to be my partner.

The training began, and we watched videos, answered questions and made notes. I carefully listed the mnemonic for giving first aid: D-R-S-A-B-C-D and noted what each letter stood for.

During a section about burns, scalds and poisons, my mind drifted away, and I imagined being on the marine rescue boat with my crewmates, crashing through the waves, speeding to assist some unfortunate soul who'd been blown out to sea, or fallen overboard. This was my new life, and I couldn't wait to be back on the water.

"And where would you find a supply of that, Shiraz?" asked Murph.

My dream of heroism evaporated in a puff of reality. "Um, supply of what, Murph? Sorry, I didn't quite catch what you said."

"A supply of saline, to induce vomiting in a case of poisoning."

"Um, saline?"

"Yes. Salt water. Where, on board a boat, miles away from the shore, are we going to find a large, let's say limitless supply of salt water?"

Emily nudged me and whispered, "The sea."

I poked her back. "All right, I was going to say that. The sea," I called, grinning.

"Correct. The sea. If we come across a case where someone has swallowed poison a long way from land, we can tell them to swallow salt water to induce vomiting. The stomach reacts to the excess of sodium chloride, or salt, and causes the patient to throw up. Note that we should use this treatment with caution. Vomiting can create more harm than the poison itself, but when you're out to sea, out of reach of a hospital, salt water's an abundant and easy option."

I leant towards Emily and whispered, "Thank you."

"No problem," she said. "You were miles away."

"It's now time for the practical part of tonight's training," said Murph. "Buddy up in pairs, one experienced crew with each new person. The first thing we'll do is practise bandaging each other. Shiraz, could you come to the front, and I'll demonstrate how we use a roller bandage to protect an open wound or a joint."

While I acted as Murph's hospital mannequin, the other crew members paired up. Boots appeared under Murph's table and somehow managed to catch his claw in the bandage being wrapped around my knee, which delayed proceedings.

"Emily," shouted Murph. "Could you please remove your cat? Put him outside."

"He's not my cat, Murph. He's Redcliff Marine Rescue's communal cat. And he lives here."

"Not during first aid training he doesn't."

Emily grabbed me after training. She held Boots in her arms. "D'you want to pop in for a bedtime cup of tea?"

"No, thanks; I'm getting an early night. We've a big day tomorrow."

"No problem. See you here at closing time."

"Yep. Goodnight."

I marched home along the seafront. The wind fluffed my hair, and the sound of ripples came from the pebble beach.

Tomorrow, Shiraz, you and your team are going to solve this little murder.

Whoever it was that killed Kateryna is not going to get away with it.

Not on my watch.

"Coffee, Shiraz? While the machine's still on."

"Yes, please. Double shot skinny latte. Same as usual."

"Oscar? For you?"

"Earl Grey tea, please. No milk. Coffee keeps me awake if I drink it in the afternoon."

"No problem. Would you like a piece of quiche each? There's some left over; it won't keep until tomorrow."

We sat at a table in the Wicked Whelk. The last customers had finished their lunches, and Emily cleared away. She brought the coffees and the quiche on small plates together with a selection of square cakes: apple, custard and chocolate flavour.

"Gosh," I said. "This looks amazing. It's a good job Alexandra Flaxworth-Mills isn't here. She'd polish off the lot."

We giggled, and Oscar furrowed his brow, then rummaged in his pocket.

"D'you recall that piece of paper you found in the collecting tin?"

"The one about devils?" asked Emily.

"Yes. The devil's factory is in Jerusalem."

"That's it," I said. "Have you figured it out?"

"My wife and I put our heads together. As I think I told you, I enjoy a cryptic crossword, and she attends the local parish church. I was staring at the paper over dinner, scratching my head, trying to work it out. She suggested that 'Jerusalem' could refer to a hymn called 'Jerusalem' which they sometimes sing at services. She tugged her hymnbook from a bookcase, and we looked through the verses."

Oscar pulled a maroon-coloured, hardback book from his pocket. He opened it at a bookmarked page.

"This was a long shot, mind you. Anyway, we racked our brains, and I think we solved it. What's another name for devil?"

"Lucifer," I said.

"Yes, but not that one."

"Satan," said Emily.

"Right." Oscar pointed at a line in the hymnbook.

We leant over and read it.

Among those dark satanic mills.

"Satan's another word for devil. Mills is another word for factories." Oscar tapped the paper. "The devil's factory. The satanic mills. D'you see?"

I gasped. "Are you implying...?"

"Yes, exactly. Somebody's sending us a message; giving us a clue. And I think I know what it...

BANG

The café door whammed open, and in walked the last person I would've expected to see.

"Sorry, we're closed," said Emily, standing. "I forgot to turn the sign around."

My hand covered my mouth, and I stared at the woman who'd walked in.

"Shiraz Jones, is that you?" she asked. "Oh my golly gosh; we thought you'd disappeared from the face of the planet. What on earth are you doing here?"

"Goodness, I could ask you the same. I certainly didn't expect to encounter you in Redcliff-upon-Sea, Victoria Harrington."

CHAPTER TWENTY-EIGHT

I stood and air-kissed Victoria on both cheeks, then realised how easy it would be for me to slip back into my two-faced, hypocritical city life, should I desire.

"Victoria, these are my friends, Emily and Oscar."

"Really?" She sniffed. "What's become of the old Shiraz we knew and loved?"

Loved? I don't think so.

She addressed Emily. "A decaf soy flat white, an espresso macchiato and a piccolo latte. Double shot in the macchiato. And make them quick. We're on a schedule."

Emily stood and glared at me. "Are these friends of yours?"

"Um, I know them, yes. Do you recognise Victoria?"

She glanced up at her. "Is she the one...?"

"Yep. From the cover of *Red Carpet Superstars*."

Emily gasped. "Oh my goodness. A food influencer. In the Wicked Whelk." She turned to Victoria. "They won't be long. D'you want anything to eat? No charge. On the house." She sprinted into the kitchen, and I heard the coffee machine fire up.

Victoria sat at a neighbouring table with her two male companions. Both wore trendy, square glasses, and they had closely cropped dark beards with hairstyles where one side of the fringe was longer than the other. One set down an expensive-looking camera with a long, white lens; the other brandished an iPad with a black stylus.

Oscar nodded at them and munched his cake.

"I'm doing a shoot for *Gourmet Affaires* magazine," said Victoria, slipping off her Armani coat and looking around to see if anyone was going to hang it up for her. She decided they weren't and folded it on her lap. "They're producing an article about seafood, and they wanted shots of me with rustic fishing boats. Something to do with the origins of the produce we eat. I can't stand the smell of these docks myself, but I suffer for my art."

Art? Commission more like.

"Um, yes. We saw you on the front cover of *Red Carpet Superstars* magazine."

"Did you like it? I thought they captured my best side. The dress was a little passé, darling, but that was the look the editor wanted. I have a copy if you'd like another look." She delved into her handbag.

Emily set down a tray of coffees. "One decaf soy flat white, one double shot espresso macchiato and one piccolo latte. And a selection of cakes."

"I thought you didn't have soy," I whispered.

"Shh. I don't."

Emily sat opposite Oscar, as Victoria pulled out the edition we'd seen in Kateryna's room and again at Alexandra Flaxworth-Mills' house.

She opened the magazine. "See? I'd have preferred it if they used one of these photos for the front cover." She opened a double-page spread near the centre which displayed several photos of Victoria reclining on a sofa, Victoria leaning on an expensive-looking kitchen counter, Victoria sitting on a balcony overlooking a city square. In each one she was wearing an outfit that looked completely unsuitable for the activity she was engaged in.

"Could I look?" asked Emily.

"Here. Keep it. I have several." Victoria slid the magazine over to her.

"Of course," said Victoria, "the more famous I become, the more paparazzi try to fire off a freebie. I have to keep the blinds drawn at home now; the other day I caught one of those parasites hiding behind a bush in my garden. Shocking."

"Stalkers," I said. "I suffered the attentions of one of them last year."

Emily crashed the magazine down in front of me. "Shiraz, you have to see this. Look."

"What?"

She tapped her finger on one of the smaller images, part of a double-page collage of wealthy young people enjoying themselves at a function. "Look who it is."

I felt a shiver run through me from top to bottom and gasped.

I lifted up the magazine.

I peered at the photo.

The figure on the left was Charlie Bramhall. He wore a black tuxedo, a white dress shirt, and he held a champagne flute in one hand.

He grinned perfect teeth and had his arm around the waist of the figure on the right, pulling her towards him so their bodies touched. A very pretty, young lady, with a stunning, hairdresser-fresh, blonde wave. She smiled too, but her smile appeared forced.

She wore a shimmering, silvery-white dress which clung to her body and flowed down to a pair of pink, killer, fashionable heels.

She also held a champagne glass, and around her throat hung a necklace with diamonds arranged in a star shape.

I looked closer and wished I had the magnifying glass with me now.

The figure-hugging robe completely failed to disguise something.

Something any woman would observe.

Something she'd been able to conceal in a winter coat, sprinting up a cliff path.

A small, oval bump in front of her.

Charlie Bramhall had his arm around Kateryna.

CHAPTER TWENTY-NINE

The caption under the photo stated: *Well-known socialite and cryptocurrency heir Charlie Bramhall with an unknown friend. He wouldn't be led on her identity, but we believe the couple are expecting a new arrival in the next few months. Watch out for a future* Red Carpet Superstars *article featuring Charlie's family.*

I jumped to my feet. "Emily. We have to leave. Now. D'you have your car keys? Take us to Redcliff Manor immediately. Bring the magazine. I know who killed Kateryna. And right now, Mrs Kilpatrick's in grave danger."

Emily jumped up and dangled the keys to the Morris Minor.

I pointed at Oscar. "Come with us. Quick. We need to hurry."

"I say," said Victoria, waggling her cup. "Another coffee?"

"Of course," said Emily. "Soy milk again?"

I grabbed her arm. "We don't have time for this, food influencer or not. She'll only review the Wicked Whelk if you pay her."

I turned to Victoria. "Make it yourself. Or tell one of your minions to do it. And close the door when you're finished."

I squeezed into the back seat to allow Oscar to hop in the front. "Quick, Emily. Don't worry about dropping the roof."

She started the engine, and we lurched away.

"That was Kateryna in the magazine, right?" shouted Emily. She crunched gears and swung around a bend into the bottom of the High Street.

"Yep. Charlie Bramhall's the father. He must've given her the dress, shoes and necklace to wear and taken her to the city to show her off. Gosh, she looked different in that magazine. Stunning."

"So who killed her, and why?"

She accelerated, and we sped through the town centre.

"We know Alexandra had the hots for Charlie. And we know, whatever brief fling they may've had, Charlie didn't have the hots for her. We also know that Alexandra reads *Red Carpet Superstars*. She would've seen the photo of Charlie and Kateryna, noticed Kateryna was pregnant, read the caption and put two and two together."

"You're saying she killed her to eliminate the competition?"

We swerved around left and right bends and shot out of the built-up area into the winding lane towards Alnchurch and the turning to Redcliff Manor.

"Exactly. She could stomach Charlie's little teenage dalliances. They meant nothing to him, and she permitted them. But there was no way she was going to put up with a pretty blonde living in Charlie's family home, who was not only clearly having an affair with Charlie but also pregnant with his child, the heir to the Bramhall fortune."

I leant forward between the front seats. "She must've befriended Kateryna, maybe enticed her with a promise of working on her stud farm or riding her horses; we know Kateryna loved horses. Did you observe a notable absence from that dinner at The King's Arms? Alexandra. She wasn't on the guest list. She knew Grantley and Charlie Bramhall would be at the event, accompanied by Nigel. She must've visited Redcliff Manor during the evening, bopped Kateryna over the head with the poker from the hall and thrown her over the cliff. No more Kateryna, no more pregnancy, now Grantley's plan can reach fruition and the two can get married."

Emily indicated, and we held on to anything available as she cornered into the lane leading to the manor.

"How would she have entered the house?" asked Oscar.

"Mrs Kilpatrick would've known her. All she had to do was announce she was there to see Kateryna, and Mrs Kilpatrick would've let her in."

"So why didn't Mrs Kilpatrick tell anyone Alexandra met with Kateryna the night she was murdered?"

"Maybe she has. It's taken until today for that someone to decipher the clues."

"Ooh," said Emily. "D'you mean us?"

"Exactly. I think Mrs Kilpatrick left us some pointers, such as the note in the money box."

"Why would she do that?" asked Oscar. "Why not come out and tell us? We don't know any of this for certain."

We skidded to a halt on Redcliff Manor's gravel drive, alongside Grantley's Rolls Royce, Charlie's red Ferrari and a vintage Jaguar.

"Then let's go inside and make it certain."

CHAPTER THIRTY

Nigel answered the door, and we burst in.

"What?" he blustered. "I've already made a donation. You can't just push your way in here and..."

"Where is she?" I asked.

"Who?"

"Alexandra Flaxworth-Mills. I know she's here; her car's outside."

"Taking tea with us. But..."

I marched past him into the room across the hall from the study. Nigel followed, and Emily and Oscar brought up the rear. In the living room, Mrs Kilpatrick and Grantley sat opposite Charlie and Alexandra, who posed with a cup of tea to her lips.

"How frightfully delightful," she squeaked. "My friends from Marine Rescue. I didn't know you knew the Bramhalls. Welcome to our little tea party." She held up a plate which contained a solid, circular, dark-brown fruit cake. A quarter of it was missing, and three small plates with crumbs on them betrayed who'd eaten. Grantley, Nigel and Mrs Kilpatrick had each consumed a slice. Alexandra, unexpectedly, hadn't had any.

I stood with my feet planted apart and my hands on my hips. "There's nothing delightful about this tea party, Alexandra Flaxworth-Mills, or should I call you 'The Satanic Mills'?"

"I don't know what you're talking about. Is this some kind of murder mystery game? I simply love those."

"There's no game about this murder mystery, is there, Alexandra?"

"Whatever d'you mean?" She linked her arm with Charlie's and shuffled closer to him. He recoiled.

Grantley Bramhall stared at me as if I were a visiting alien. "Get out. Unless you leave immediately, I'm calling the police."

"Go ahead. Call the police. It won't be me they'll arrest. It'll be her." I pointed at Alexandra with my outstretched arm. "She was so desperate to marry Charlie, she wouldn't let anything, or anyone stand in her way. Oh, yes, you overlooked Charlie's little teenage flings, didn't you?"

Charlie turned a beetroot colour and shrank into his jacket.

"But you couldn't overlook his relationship with the attractive, live-in stable hand. And I'll bet he never bought you a dress like this, did he? Show them, Emily."

Emily turned around the page of the *Red Carpet Superstars* magazine and demonstrated it to everyone in the room as if she were an auctioneer's assistant showing off a valuable painting. She pointed at Kateryna's bump, perfectly silhouetted against the backdrop of the photo. "Exhibit A."

"Who's the father of that little bump in there?" I demanded. "Who so enraged Alexandra's passion and jealousy that she felt compelled to commit murder? Who was it?"

I pointed at Mrs Kilpatrick. "Tell them, Mrs Kilpatrick. Tell everybody, who is the father of Kateryna's baby?"

Everyone remained in stunned silence and stared at Joan Kilpatrick.

The old lady blinked, her skin turned grey, and she fell sideways.

"She's fainted." Emily grasped Mrs Kilpatrick under the armpits and propped her up. "Somebody help me."

Alexandra's face changed to an evil, dare I say it, satanic, expression I hadn't seen before. "You're too late." Her finger pointed at the fruit cake. "She hasn't fainted. She's dying. Horse tranquiliser in the baking. The old housekeeper's the first to succumb." She stood, tossed her hair, grinned unpleasantly, grabbed a metal candlestick and threatened me with it. "I already disposed of the foreign girl. Maybe you want to be next?"

I leapt at Alexandra, and she fell backwards as we collided. The candlestick flew out of her hand and smashed into a painting of a buxom Elizabethan with a spaniel on her lap.

"Oscar, Charlie," I shouted. "Help me restrain her."

Oscar tugged out the long curtain ropes, and while he held her arms down, Charlie tied her feet.

"Ooh," said Alexandra. "I never knew you were into tying me up. We could've had such spiffing fun, the two of us. What a shame these people had to butt in on our love-nest."

"Tie her hands," I yelled. "Sit on her. Don't let her escape. Emily, find salt in the kitchen and make a saline solution. We need to induce vomiting in anyone who's eaten the fruit cake. Oscar, call an ambulance. And the police."

Alexandra jabbed her finger at me. "When I saw that foreigner in the magazine with the baby bump that's supposed to be mine, I knew she had to go. She's paid for her sins, the hussy. My Charlie and me, we'll live here at Redcliff Manor forever and make lots of little Charlies and Alexandras, won't we, my love?"

"You'll have plenty of time to fantasise in prison," I said. "You were never going to be anything but a one-night stand."

Nigel began to choke, and Grantley doubled up, holding his stomach.

"Oscar, make that two ambulances."

I knelt in front of Mrs Kilpatrick, who remained unconscious, although she was breathing.

Quick, Shiraz, first aid. D—R—S—A—B—C—D. What's the first thing? D—Danger? Plenty of that here. R—Response. Shout at the patient.

"Mrs Kilpatrick, can you hear me?" I shook her shoulder. Emily administered saline solution to Grantley and Nigel.

"Mrs Kilpatrick. Don't die on me. Can you hear me? Can you hear me?"

Oscar poked his head around the door. "The first ambulance is on the way. And the police."

"Tell them to hurry. I hope it's not too late. Mrs Kilpatrick, wake up. Please. Wake up."

CHAPTER THIRTY-ONE

Three days later

"How is she?" I asked the ward nurse. "Can she receive visitors?"

"She's weak physically, but she's surprised us all with how alert her mind is. She has an opinion on everything in the news and gives us updates every day. And she's able to complete the cryptic crossword within half an hour of the newspapers being delivered. Remarkable, for a person in her eighties. It's fortunate whoever tried to poison her didn't succeed. You go on in."

She held out her arm and drew me into a room with a hospital bed, a small table and a chair.

"Mrs Kilpatrick?"

The elderly housekeeper opened her eyes. She'd aged another ten years from her ordeal, but Alexandra's fatal attraction hadn't claimed another victim, thank goodness.

"Mrs Kilpatrick? It's Shiraz. D'you remember me?"

I sat on the visitor's chair next to her bed.

"Shiraz. Lovely name. I think all of us at Redcliff Manor owe you a debt of gratitude. Especially me."

Her breaths came quick and shallow.

"How are you feeling?" I asked.

"I'll live. More to the point, Shiraz, how are you feeling? That was quite an achievement to put that evil woman behind bars."

She grasped my hand, and I was surprised at the strength of her grip.

"I knew it was her," she said. "I knew she was responsible for that poor girl's death."

"You mean you knew Alexandra killed Kateryna?"

"She came to visit her that Friday night. The night of Sir James Flaxworth-Mills' charity event at the King's Arms. I was immediately suspicious, as she'd only ever been to the house to see Charlie, and he was out at the dinner."

"Did Alexandra know Kateryna before?"

"I don't believe they'd ever met. I showed her into the hall and asked her to wait while I fetched Kateryna from her room above the stables. It was a cold evening; I remember I wished I'd brought a jacket as I walked across the courtyard and called up to her."

"Did Kateryna come down?"

"Yes. She had no idea what Alexandra wanted, and nor had I, until they introduced themselves in the hall. I left them alone to talk, but I was naughty." She winked. "I hid in the laundry, as I wanted to listen to their conversation."

"Goodness. What did you overhear?"

"Alexandra spun a tale about offering Kateryna a role at her stud. She flattered her, told her she'd pay her far more than Grantley did, and she'd be working with racing thoroughbreds, not Grantley's old nags. I peeked around the corner, and she was showing her this pair of silver-coloured horseshoes. Of course, I had no idea what they were. I don't know much about horses."

"Was Kateryna interested?"

"I'll say she was. Grantley and Nigel were never particularly nice to her. She wasn't happy. The only time I saw her face light up was when she met that boy, Josh."

She paused and caught her breath. I offered grapes from a chipped, ceramic bowl on the side table. She ate one, little bite by little bite.

"Alexandra asked if there was somewhere they could go to discuss this further, and Kateryna led her past my hiding place, through the kitchen and out into the yard. As fast as my old legs would carry me, I climbed the stairs and peeked from my bedroom window, from where I have a clear view of the rear entrance. I was just in time to see the gate latch behind them. The gate out to the meadows and the cliffs."

She glanced down at her lap.

"All I know is, I never saw Kateryna again, and the next thing, they found her body on West Cove. So tragic. She escaped war, and then this happened."

"Gosh," I said. "It wouldn't take much to make the connection that Alexandra had been the last person to see Kateryna alive. Did you tell the police?"

Mrs Kilpatrick shrugged. "How could I? Grantley was so desperate for Charlie to marry Alexandra and inveigle his way into her titled family, he wouldn't hear a bad word about her. I was terrified, if I divulged what I knew, and Alexandra was arrested, Grantley would turf me out. I don't need the money from housekeeping; I have a pension I can survive on, but I do need the place to live." She smoothed down the covers in front of her. "Redcliff Manor's been my home for over fifty years. I can't leave now."

She plucked a second grape from the dish and ate it slowly, then jabbed one finger at me. "And that's where you came into my plan."

"Me?" I frowned and pointed at my chest.

The old lady nodded. "I thought if I couldn't tell the police directly, I could tell someone who'd tell them. That way, Alexandra would be caught, but I couldn't be implicated in the arrest. When you visited the manor the first time, I watched you and your friend sneak across the yard and enter the stables from my upstairs bedroom window, so I wondered if you were on to something."

I shrugged. "But you didn't tell me. I worked it out, with my friends Emily and Oscar."

"Ah, yes. Oscar Wainwright, the ex-police sergeant. I was sure he'd be tangled up in this somehow. He never could calm his investigative instincts. Shiraz, I gave you four clues to help you. Although, I had no idea whether you'd work them out. I had to hope."

"Four clues?" I tapped my flat hand on my mouth. "D'you mean the message in the money box?"

"That was one of them. Clever, don't you think? I surmised you were an intelligent girl. I figured you'd work that one out in the end."

"Gosh, it was very cryptic. That took four minds to solve: mine, Emily's, Oscar's and his wife's."

I squinted as I turned memories over in my mind. "The second and third clues were the horseshoes?"

"Correct. I found the two horseshoes on the hall table after Alexandra and Kateryna's meeting. At the same time, I noticed the poker was missing, but I never discovered what happened to that."

"I found it. On West Cove beach."

"Ah. So that was the murder weapon. I thought it must've been. Anyway, the first horseshoe, I slipped into Charlie's coat pocket while he was busy entertaining one of his girlfriends. I had no idea what I hoped to achieve by that, or if you'd ever find it, so I had to take more blatant action with the second one."

I gasped. "You threw the horseshoe through my window?" I stared at Mrs Kilpatrick. I hadn't realised she had the stamina to leave the house and walk all the way through the town, let alone smash a window.

"Of course I didn't. I'm too elderly to be doing those kinds of things. A young ruffian called at the manor one day, asking for money. I told him I'd pay him handsomely if he'd break a window for me. Obviously, he thought that a strange request, but when he saw the bundle of notes I offered him, he didn't hesitate. I'm so sorry about your window. Please, let me pay for it."

"It's all good. The coxswain at Marine Rescue's a glazier. He fixed it for me."

"I rather hoped the horseshoe clues would lead directly to her."

"We eventually made the connection." I paused. "You mentioned four clues. What was the fourth?" I grasped the chipped, ceramic platter, tugged a small bunch of grapes from it and handed them to Mrs Kilpatrick.

"The cat's water bowl. You're holding it. I asked the same ruffian to pinch something that could only have come from the café. I knew you'd been to the manor twice, and I figured if I placed the bowl in the hallway, the next time you visited you'd have some questions about why an item from the café was there. This wasn't an obvious clue, and you never came back, so that plan didn't work. Imagine how surprised I was when Mr Bramhall brought me grapes in it. Please take it back. Tell Emily I'm sorry. And sorry to her cat."

"It's okay. We solved the mystery in the end. With the help of one or two of your clues and a piece of luck."

I paused. "There's one thing I don't understand about all this. When I first met Kateryna, she told me she was pregnant. She said she was ashamed, and her family could never know. She even threatened suicide. Why was she so distraught about carrying Charlie Bramhall's baby? I know they're not married, and from very different backgrounds, but surely in this day and age…?"

Mrs Kilpatrick frowned. "Charlie Bramhall? Kateryna had a brief affair with him; it's true. But he wasn't the father."

"Really? Who was? You told me you knew."

"Kateryna was pregnant when she arrived at Redcliff Manor. She was a Ukrainian refugee, remember. She came to me in tears when she saw her pregnancy test result. She could never have told her family the identity of the father, not with her brother being killed in the war. And I quite understand why she felt suicidal."

Mrs Kilpatrick paused, glanced up at me and met my eyes. "Shiraz, Kateryna's baby was fathered by a Russian soldier."

CHAPTER THIRTY-TWO

"Tonight," announced Murph the following evening, "you've completed the final part of basic training."

I spotted Boots eyeing up the laptop out of the corner of my eye and wondered whether he'd jump on the keyboard again and disrupt the presentation.

Murph continued. "We've covered safety equipment and clothing, tides and local hazards and behaviour on the boat, both academically and practically. Some of you have taken part in running a search pattern, a taste of what you could experience as you progress through your marine rescue careers."

Emily and I glanced at each other and smiled. We'd practised a search pattern more than once, although Murph didn't know that.

"And, finally, you've all passed your first aid training. All of you are now permitted to go out with a skipper and qualified crew member on general duty days, liaise with the public and, if necessary, offer assistance when we get a shout. Remember, though, you're not fully certified crew yet, and you shouldn't attempt anything you're not trained for."

Together with the other three new recruits, we clapped and cheered.

"Do we get a graduation certificate?" Emily asked Murph.

He winked. "Do I get a bacon sandwich?"

"Maybe. Come to the Wicked Whelk tomorrow morning."

We stood and gathered our possessions.

"Oh, Murph," I said, "before we go, I forgot to give this back to you." I handed him the collection tin which we'd reassembled.

He cracked it open, and Nigel's coin rolled out. "Walloping whipstaffs. One copper coin? Is that it? I told you pickings were slim in winter."

"Sorry, Murph. We'll try again in the warmer months."

David entered, and I glanced downward and smiled.

"Hi, Emily. Hi, Shiraz," he said. "Basic training complete? It'll be great to have more women on the crew, won't it, Murph?"

"It will, David. So long as you don't become distracted."

Emily, Oscar and I sat around a table at the Smuggler's Tavern, a seafront pub with a panoramic view of Redcliff Bay.

"I don't get invited out for a drink very often," said Emily. "This is a pleasant drop."

"Châteauneuf-du-Pape." I topped their glasses up. "I'm ashamed to say I consumed a lot of it in my city life."

"Whoever would've thought Alexandra Flaxworth-Mills could be a murderer?" asked Oscar. "Her father's employed a PR company to manage the fallout. So far, they've succeeded in keeping it off the front pages."

"If it's the PR company I'm thinking of, they're pretty good at that."

"So, what for you now, Shiraz?" asked Oscar. "Will you build your detective agency further, or return to civilian life?"

I laughed. "The first thing I need to do is find somewhere to live. I'm supposed to be out of Melville Cottage this weekend, and all this investigating has stopped me from looking for somewhere more permanent."

"Why don't you stay with me?" asked Emily.

"Really? Above the Wicked Whelk?"

"Of course. I have a spare bedroom, although it's full of supplies. We can clear it out."

"That'd be great. How much should I pay you?"

"Nothing. I'd love your company."

"I can't pay you nothing. How about I help out in the café when it's busy? You said you needed someone."

"A perfect result," said Oscar.

"Indeed. I'm looking forward to gaining my qualified crew certificate, slotting into Redcliff life and not becoming involved in any more murder investigations."

"Let's drink to that," said Emily, and we clinked glasses.

SHIRAZ'S ADVENTURES CONTINUE IN BOOK 2:
A DEADLY AFFAIR IN THE PIRATE'S LAIR

SHIRAZ'S NEXT ADVENTURE

Hi, it's Simon.

Thank you so much for reading *A Murderous Clamour at Redcliff Manor*, the first in my *Shiraz Jones Marine Rescue Mysteries* series.

If you'd like to read more of Shiraz's adventures in Redcliff, why not:

Sign up for my newsletter at simonmichaelprior.com

Follow me on Amazon to be notified of new releases.

And please consider leaving a review to let other readers know how much you enjoyed it. A few words will suffice. Even if you didn't buy the book from Amazon, you can still leave a review there if you have a valid Amazon account. I read every one with interest and gratitude.

Now, if you wish, you could continue directly onto *Shiraz Jones Marine Rescue Mysteries* book two:

A Deadly Affair in the Pirate's Lair

Available from Amazon and all good bookshops.

MORE BOOKS BY SIMON

Available on Amazon and from all good bookshops

Shiraz Jones Marine Rescue Mysteries

A Murderous Clamour at Redcliff Manor

A Deadly Affair in the Pirate's Lair

A Landslide, a Bride and a Fatal Ride

Fun Travel Memoirs

The Coconut Wireless:
A Travel Adventure in Search of the Queen of Tonga

The Scenicland Radio:
A Travel Adventure in Search of the New Zealand Experience

The Pomegranate Busker:
A Travel Adventure in Search of New Zealand Rock Stardom

The Anticlockwise Proposal:
A Travel Adventure Around the World in Eighty Diamonds

A Capybara for Christmas:
European Travel, Japanese Adventure, Maximum Mayhem

Historical Memoirs

An Englishman in New York:
The Memoirs of John Miskin Prior 1948-1949

DISCLAIMER

A Murderous Clamour at Redcliff Manor is a work of fiction, based on the experiences of Simon Michael Prior, a search and rescue skipper with one of the many volunteer marine rescue organisations seafarers depend on.

Although the book is set in England, the town of Redcliff-upon-Sea and the surrounding locations are fictional. Redcliff Marine Rescue is a fictional organisation. Montague Jones PR Ltd is a fictional company. *Red Carpet Superstars* magazine is a fictional publication. Which is a shame, as it sounds like a good read.

Names, characters, places and incidents are either products of the author's imagination or are used fictitiously. Any resemblance to actual events or locales or persons, living or dead, is entirely coincidental.

I had to say that.

ACKNOWLEDGEMENTS

This book wouldn't have been possible without the help of the following people: The wonderful beta readers: Alyson Sheldrake, Dawne Archer, Lisa Rose Wright, Louise Pierce, Timothy Morral, Rebecca Hislop and Val Poore; your feedback improved the final result so much.

Thank you to Nicholas Thresher for ensuring Shiraz's interactions with paramedics were medically accurate.

Thank you to Victoria Twead, Matthew J Holmes, Meg LaTorre, Craig Martelle, Angela Ackerman, Becca Puglisi, David Gaughran and Dave Chesson for informative courses, tips and useful tools.

Thank you to Jeff Bezos, for giving independent authors a platform on which to publish our writing.

And thank you so much to the skippers and crew of the AVCGA Volunteer Coastguard. I couldn't have done it without you.

ABOUT THE AUTHOR

Simon Michael Prior experiences constant adventures, hazards and exciting situations as a marine rescue skipper and a commander of rescue operations.

Although Simon is absolutely nothing like Murph, Redcliff Marine Rescue's burly, grumpy coxswain, many of the scenes in his stories are inspired by events he encounters during his duties.

Simon has also lived on two boats and sunk one of them; sold houses, street signs, Indian food and paper bags for a living; visited almost fifty countries and lived in three; qualified as a scuba diving instructor; nearly killed himself learning to wakeboard and built his own house without the benefit of an instruction manual.

He now lives in it by the sea with his wife and twin daughters, where he spends his time regurgitating his experiences on paper before he has so many more that he forgets them.

Website and newsletter sign up: simonmichaelprior.com
Email: simon@simonmichaelprior.com
Facebook: @simonmichaelprior
Instagram: @simonmichaelprior